Seven Days to Heaven

C.T. Fox and L.R. Bennett

authorHOUSE®

AuthorHouse™
1663 Liberty Drive
Bloomington, IN 47403
www.authorhouse.com
Phone: 1-800-839-8640

First published by AuthorHouse   9/28/2010

ISBN: 978-1-4520-7345-3 (e)
ISBN: 978-1-4520-7344-6 (sc)

Printed in the United States of America

This book is printed on acid-free paper.

Contents

Chapter One
"The Unexpected"

Ext. Rooftop. Dusk (Present Day)

As I sit here on this rooftop bleeding tremendously and breathing faintly, I know I have but a few minutes to live before I fade to black. I can't help but to wonder why I was even born. Me being a strong athletic afro American, it's not that I hated life; I just didn't want to live to see this. I'm content now, but the Bible says, "Thou shall not kill" so Lord please forgive me. Mercy is not mine to give right now, and I must have my revenge down to my last breath.

It's funny, just last Saturday at 11:45 p.m. almost seven days to the hour, my life had made an unexpected but welcomed change, but good things never last long. Before last Saturday, my life smelled worse than all of the stench of the blood and decaying flesh around me. Then, I remember this dream that I had. This girl came to me and told me who she was and what I meant to God. Never did I think that I would actually meet this woman.

Looking down I see the slaughter in the street. I can hear them coming. It doesn't matter now; I have nothing left to live for. A few days ago I had nothing left to die for. Well, there's no light at the end of this tunnel for me, not Senar. As I look back at these last days, I still don't believe it. Just when I thought things couldn't get any worse, the guy I needed to see gets shot in front of my house selling to a crack head.

That's why I hate the holidays; people get depressed about everything they don't have, forgetting about what they've got. I decided to get to Blair's house early. He said he needed help cooking something his sister might like. I didn't know what he meant, but I was sure going to find out. When I got there, my man Keith tried to sell me things that I don't need. That's the devil for you. If I knew then what I know now, at least I could have been sedated. Blair was a tall broad shoulder man who needed a ride to the airport to pick up his sister. I was curious anyway so I said come on. Wow! I should've stayed home. Anyia was her name, 5' 11", 160 lbs., sandy brown hair and copper brown skin. Her lips weren't bad either. You could tell she was from the Islands and you could also tell she was Blair's sister by her features. She had a nice tan and a very vivacious voice, so after our introductions we went back to the house and fired up the grill. While Blair pulled the TV outside, you could tell something was on Anyia's mind. It was like she was here but not because she wanted to be.

Day One

Ext. Backyard. Day

V.O. – Kids playing, adults' playing cards, teenagers jump roping, people dancing.

SENAR: What's up? I hope I'm not interrupting.

BLAIR: You hope too much.

SENAR: So Anyia, what really brings you here?

ANYIA: Love and the never ending pursuit for the truth.

BLAIR: Love for who?

ANYIA: Our father and for you.

SENAR: You don't even know him like that.

ANYIA: Blood is blood where I come from and knowing of one another is just like being there. You wouldn't understand yet.

BLAIR: What do you mean yet?

SENAR: Well all righty then. Now you're starting to get my attention. Go on. I want to know more.

BLAIR: Why do I feel like more is not better in this case?

V.O. – She and Blair sat around getting to know each other while I jumped in the conversation here and there. She was telling us about something that happened at the airport. Some guy at the airport said he needed her help. She said he had a picture of him and her father, so she went with him to his room at the hotel. She said she listened to what he had to say, while in the back of her mind she wondered if he was a serial killer. She went on to explain that the terrified look in his eyes suggested that he was telling the truth. At this point in her story, her eyes began to water, so I suggested we go play some spades or volleyball just to take our minds off of this emotional conversation. Besides, I wanted to see her relax anyway. As she began to loosen up, she asked me if I drink. I said no, but I wouldn't rule anything out today. Blair and Tommy went with Kiwi to the ABC store. Tommy was bad news and Kiwi was the queen of drama. It's nothing to be proud of, but it was who they were and they were still our friends. Anyia went on to say, "If I told you everything your life would be in danger." Bored as I was, I was dying to listen.

ANYIA: My father was the main man at Gen-Tech.

SENAR: Gen-who?

ANYIA: Gen-Tech is a government contracted company that had their hands in everything.

SENAR: Like what, if you don't mind me asking?

ANYIA: From clone technology to world defense and that's just a couple.

SENAR: Why would we need world defense technology and who are they cloning?

ANYIA: My father has been missing for over four months now, and I don't know how to tell Blair.

SENAR: Okay, it's time to drink it over.

ANYIA: I thought you quit.

SENAR: I think I better start again because I got a feeling that I'm going to need to be drunk to fully comprehend the truth. Yeah, that's it.

ANYIA: (Laughing very hard) Well, here. I guess it's alright. You seem to be responsible.

V.O. – Just when I thought things couldn't get any stranger, a black van pulled in the alley. At first I thought it was a drive by, but they sat there too long. The look in Anyia's eyes told me she knew who they were, so I began to walk toward the van, and as I got closer, my boys got up too. We were all strapped and showing. I guess this wasn't the time or the place because they pulled off before we could get a good look at them. Now it was really time to get some answers, and I knew we needed to drink to get them. Anyia, ready or not, needed to give them. I grabbed Anyia by the arm and sat her down.

SENAR: (Looking confused) Anyia, do you know them?

ANYIA: (Evasively) Yes and no.

SENAR: What are you saying?

ANYIA: I know who they are, but I don't know what they are. It's kind of hard to explain.

SENAR: Give it to me in black and white.

ANYIA: My father was into gene splicing and DNA cloning. The man at the airport was a friend of my father's. As he was starting to tell me what happened to my father, I went in the bathroom. While I was in the bathroom, I heard a knock on the front door.

SENAR: Then what?

ANYIA: When I came out, he was lying on the floor with two shots in his head.

SENAR: Un-freaking-believable. Go on.

ANYIA: In a panic, I grabbed my bag and ran out the door.

SENAR: Did you call the cops?

ANYIA: No, I drove back to the airport and went into the Burger King restroom. I reached in my bag, and there was a canister with a note attached.

SENAR: Okay, this gets better. Hold up. Pass the Jack Daniels please.

ANYIA: I thought you didn't drink?

SENAR: Yeah, whatever. Pass the Jack.

ANYIA: Here, well anyway, the note said that my father was killed because he wanted to warn the world.

SENAR: About what?

ANYIA: I don't know exactly, but it also said not to open the canister.

SENAR: Did you open it?

ANYIA: No. I'm not stupid.

Senar V.O. – As Anyia saw Blair coming, she decided to tell him the truth as she knew it and as she shared this info with me, *a* sense of calm came over me. I believe it was the Jack kicking in. I didn't know for sure, but I was really ready to change the subject. Not wanting to ruin the cookout and seeing Blair was visibly upset, I thought it was a good idea. As Blair and Kiwi went to his room, I felt it was time for me to go too.

Int. Walking Through Back Door of the House. Day

Senar V.O. – We gather in the living room trying to take our mind off of what Anyia just told us. I noticed Anyia looking out of the window constantly. I grabbed her hand and began to dance with her.

Kiwi and Blair made drinks for everyone, so we sat down to catch our breath. The euphoric mood that covered the room seemed to ease everyone's nerves. It was beginning to get late and for some that's when the real fun started.

SENAR: (Sarcastically) Well, that's my cue.

ANYIA: For what?

SENAR: To go home and drink it over.

ANYIA: You can do that here, can't you?

SENAR: Why? You want to see me at your next AA meeting?

ANYIA: (Pleading) Come on. Stay. I'm scared.

SENAR: Of what?

ANYIA: You'll see soon enough.

SENAR: Have you ever used a gun before?

ANYIA: No, but I can throw a knife pretty well.

SENAR: Okay, I'm going to show you how to use this nine. Just don't throw it when it's empty.

ANYIA: I promise.

SENAR: Just don't freak me out anymore tonight.

ANYIA: (Laughing) I can't promise you that.

SENAR: There's only one bed in here.

ANYIA: So, what's your point?

SENAR: Well all righty then.

Int. Bedroom. Night

Senar V.O. – So we forced down a few beers and went to sleep. Around 1 a.m. I went to the bathroom while trying to navigate my way through the house in the dark. Walking back to the bedroom, I noticed the kitchen door open, knowing that I locked that door. I knew something was wrong. Before I could get to the bedroom, I noticed the kitchen floor was wet, so I stopped in my tracks. Just then someone grabbed my arm and pulled me into the closet. I was about to freak until I realized it was Anyia. She said, "They're here." She handed me my gun and told me to be real quiet. As I slowly made my way through the house trying to get to Blair, I could see Kiwi in the doorway. Before I could get to her, she called out my name; then there was a flash and then brains on the wall. I fired at the figure, and then at the figure I saw at the window.

Someone returned fire and I was hit. The impact to my shoulder took me off my feet. As the figure walked towards me, my gun was no longer in my hand. When I could make out his face, what I saw was unreal. I never thought it would end this way. Good thing I already kissed my butt good-bye. As he reached out to fire at me, there was a shot and then he went down. Good thing I showed Anyia how to use the nine. I looked in Blair's room; they had already shot him execution style. Looking at the body on the floor, I guess my aim was pretty good in the dark. This was like nothing I'd ever seen before. Their bodies were decaying rapidly. Hearing the sirens in the background, this would be too hard to explain. Five bodies in a house is not a thing that you could explain away. I know when it's time for me to leave. I grabbed Blair's keys and all the guns, and ammo I could hold and ran out the back door. Anyia was right behind me with her bag and that black canister. As we went speeding through the city in a state of shock, neither of us had any words. For one moment I felt like O.J. I needed some answers, but she had just watched her brother be executed. I figured now wasn't the time. We couldn't go to the cops and couldn't go home. I drove north until we came to a motel off of 95 north. I was looking for some peace because we just needed some rest.

Chapter Two
"Reflection"

Day Two

Int. Hotel. Pre-Dawn

Senar V.O. - Once at the hotel, I began to reflect on the events of the night. Now was the time for answers and sleep was the last thing I wanted to do, but it was much needed. Anyia wanted to take a shower and under normal circumstances I would love to see her relaxing in such a way, but nothing was normal right now. As she walked to the shower, I couldn't help but notice the grace that she carried in her movements. It was as though she was a woman of great power. When she came out, she reached for the phone. I suggested that making a call could be very risky right now.

SENAR: I think you should get some rest, and I'll stand the first watch.

ANYIA: What about you?

SENAR: I'll rest when you wake up.

ANYIA: Are you sure?

SENAR: Yes, I'm sure. Go to sleep. Why are you about to cry?

ANYIA: Because it brings sadness to my heart that I cannot ease your emotional pain that you carry in your heart.

SENAR: Excuse me. Come again?

ANYIA: I brought you into something that has but one way to end.

SENAR: Yeah, and what's that?

ANYIA: There will be great suffering. Then there will be forever joy.

SENAR: What the heck are you talking about? Please tell me the truth.

ANYIA: Some things are not for us to know. There are two children that will be born and only because of the time will science have its chance to shine, but soon after Jesus will come and prove that it was all for not.

SENAR: For not what?

ANYIA: For now we depend on science for soon we will only depend on God.

SENAR: (Laughing) Get some sleep. You can tell me later, after I wake up.

Senar V.O. – As she laid there naked, I was amazed by the beauty of her body. She was almost perfect except for what looked like a birthmark on the back of her neck. I couldn't make out what it was, but it, too, was beautiful in its own way. Looking out of the window, my daughter, Toonie, came to mind. She would always say, "Look to the stars, and there you shall find me." Man, I really miss her. Me and her mom didn't see eye to eye on anything, so we went our separate ways. Toonie's mom was hard and bitter about her childhood, and she never had too much respect for anyone, so I knew she wouldn't have any for me, but I married her anyway. I wish things could have been different between us, but nothing turns out the way you want it. Toonie blames me for me and her mom not making it and she believed everything her mama told her about me, even though some of it is true. Maybe one day I could find someone that I could trust with all my deepest secrets, but love is not found in the want ads and for someone to truly understand me; they would have to be from another planet. I must be tripping to even think that person could exist.

V.O. – Senar reflecting back to a dream he had when he was seven years old, about a woman coming to him in his nightmare saving him from the demons that were pulling at his flesh. For so long he could never make out her face, but he couldn't help but to notice that she looked a lot like Anyia.

Int. Bathroom. Early Morning

V.O. – Anyia wakes up. Walks into the bathroom where Senar is standing looking in the mirror.

ANYIA: (Joyfully) Hey, good looking. How did you sleep?

SENAR: Oh! You got jokes too, huh?

ANYIA: Are you hungry?

SENAR: Food would help a tad bit.

ANYIA: Here! I had these sandwiches on the plane. They're a bit soggy.

SENAR: That's cool, I like soggy.

ANYIA: Oh really now?

SENAR: Stop playing. It's not time to play.

Senar V.O. – Just when I thought we could relax, all hell breaks out. People were running away from the hotel. I figured that couldn't be a good thing. As I looked out the window,

I could see people dead in the street and all who were not dead were running. Waiting to see what it was that was chasing them, I told Anyia to get dressed, grab her stuff, and head towards the window. As I opened the window, one of those "what the hells" was standing right there. So I shot it in the face, grabbed Anyia and headed through the woods off the main highway. We ran until we came to a lake. On the other side of the lake was a house. I didn't see them, but I knew they couldn't be far behind. We had to get back to the city. I figured we had a better chance there. We circled the lake until we came to a road. The road was directly behind the house we saw before. There was an old pickup truck in the garage, so I hot-wired it and took off flying up the road. Just as we thought we were safe, shots rang out. I was hit again, but this time it wasn't a flesh wound. It went straight through my right side. I struggled to keep control and I managed to make it to the highway and pulled over. Now I was hot; I got out and returned fire all behind us. We heard a loud screech or scream, whatever, but it didn't sound good. Anyia got in the driver's seat, and I jumped in on the passenger side. I was bleeding pretty badly, so time was a factor for me.

Anyia decides not to head toward the city, she begins to head upstate. Anyia was concerned about my well being and told me that I would have to trust her. Me knowing that there was a cross road about five miles ahead, I had to make a choice. The city was straight down to the right, our last chance, but Anyia wanted to go left.

Ext. Truck. Back Road. Day

Senar V.O. - As she stopped at the cross road, she looked at me as though this was my last chance.

ANYIA: We all must come to a crossroad sometime in life, and it just happens to be your turn. Now, I need you to trust me to make this decision for you.

SENAR: What! It's simple. Go to the closest hospital.

ANYIA: There may not be anyone there.

SENAR: Oh, right, well okay. I remember when I was little, my mamma used to always tell me that sometimes in life you were going to come to a crossroad and which way you go, comes down to nothing but faith, so do your thing.

ANYIA: Let me stop the bleeding. I found some rags and some Jack Daniels.

SENAR: Give me the Jack.

ANYIA: Here you go. Now give it back, so I can sterilize the wound. Be still.

SENAR: Man! That hurts!

ANYIA: Do you trust me?

SENAR: Yes, my life is in yours and the Lord's hands.

Senar V.O. - Anyia looked like the decision she was about to make was one that would have everlasting impact. She started to put the Jack up, but she took a good swig. Let me tie it up, she said as though she needed not to panic me. After she patched me up, it got real quiet in the truck.

SENAR: What's the matter? Do you hear something?

ANYIA: Yeah, where is I-95?

SENAR: East always east.

ANYIA: We're going north. It's safe to say that the roads and highways are being watched.

SENAR: I'm getting dizzy here.

ANYIA: You're losing too much blood. I'm gonna take you to a friend's house upstate. She'll take care of you. It's only a two and a half hour drive. Just hang on.

SENAR: Do I have a choice?

ANYIA: (Laughing) Yes, you can jump out and walk back to the hotel.

SENAR: You got jokes while I'm dying here. Okay, that's love.

Chapter Three
"Crossroad"

Ext. Lab. Day

SEANR V.O. - By now I had lost a lot of blood trusting Anyia, but we finally reached our destination. I figured we were about a hundred miles or so northwest of the city. It's a big white house fenced in with a guard shack and everything. Two of her friends, came out of the house as we pulled up to the guard shack. They motioned to the guards to let us through, and they did just that. These friends of hers said hello then immediately sedated me. I woke up several hours later to find myself in a high tech lab. Extremely confused, I tried to get up, but I was too drowsy from the medication. I could see an extremely worried look on everyone's faces as though they just found out something they didn't want to know. Anyia helped me up and took me upstairs to introduce me to Shelia, a corn-fed country girl with Portuguese background whose mother was a genius in genetic science. They sat me down to explain what was really going on.

SHELIA: There's no need to keep a secret anymore. Anyia and I are part of a secret society whose goal is to uncover the greatest secret ever kept.

SENAR: What's that?

ANYIA: Shelia and I may share one secret among men, but we all share a promise my Lord has made too and soon even the secret of man won't matter.

SHELIA: Ok Anyia, only one thing at a time and I am not really sure what you're talking about now. Are you talking about the President cloning his dead daughter?

ANYIA: No! I'm sorry go ahead.

SHELIA: Well, it's like this. What Anyia has in the canister is positive proof of extraterrestrials and that life does exist on other planets.

SENAR: Right, just what I wanted to hear. Okay, give me my gun. I'm outta here.

SHELIA: Wait. There's more.

SENAR: How come I knew you was going to say that?

ANYIA: Please, Senar, listen to her. If you trust me, please give her a chance to explain.

SHELIA: In an earlier shuttle mission, our labs were responsible for sending samples of various viruses to space to see if what and if any mutations would take place.

SENAR: What happened?

ANYIA: I recovered the sample which was brought back to us, three people have disappeared and basically Shelia and I know where they are.

SHELIA: In two or three samples, the virus was attacked by a biological life form which is capable of mimicking the DNA structure or genetic code of whatever it comes in contact with.

ANYIA: Seeing the capabilities of this certain military and political interest deemed it valuable.

SENAR: I want to know how is it you feel that I have anything to contribute to this at all.

SHELIA: In a rush to uncover the mystery, certain individuals were exposed to the virus. Seeing the effects on these unwilling participants, the excitement grew.

ANYIA: In conjunction with our government gene splicing program, various experiments resulted in tragedy. A whole underground lab in NW Nevada was slaughtered.

SHELIA: One thousand people, the total work population, their families have yet to be told.

ANYIA: Being that this just happened, they were told that they are on assignment.

SENAR: This is crazy.

ANYIA: Doing more research, we found out that the cow mutilations were part of an earlier government exchange with life forms first contacted in Roswell.

SHELIA: The deal was in exchange for high tech technology beyond our common sense, we agreed to help.

SENAR: Help do what?

SHELIA: Incubate and regenerate their population.

ANYIA: This includes abductions of men, women, and children by them and our governments worldwide.

SHELIA: While using these people for experiments, they began to evolve into a hybrid version of people, animals and any creature they chose to be.

SENAR: Can I have a drink?

SHELIA: Sure.

SENAR: Anyia, please give me my jacket.

ANYIA: Why?

SENAR: Please!

ANYIA: Here you go. What's that?

SENAR: The Jack I had earlier.

SHELIA: (Laughing) Let him have it. He probably needs it about now. Years later other life forms were contacted, but with more extreme measures in mind.

ANYIA: In the Regan Administration, a war was supported by backing the Contras. Our government has documented reports of Contra Rebels that their enemy was being slaughtered by creatures that they had never seen before. World leaders realized that these life forms had come with hostile intent.

SENAR: Please pass me the bottle.

ANYIA: Sure.

SENAR: Thank you. Well all righty then.

SHELIA: Star Wars was created as a defense against these hostiles, while dealing with the exterior threat and the interior threat now herding us like cattle.

ANYIA: That's almost everything, some things you will come to find out in time.

SENAR: Don't wait until the last minute.

SHELIA: The story Anyia told you about the man at the hotel was true, only she knew he would be there. Anyia has been working for us since she was a child following her father around the lab.

ANYIA: The contents of that canister are the only thing that may save us from extinction as a result of our private ventures.

SHELIA: Funded by us alone.

ANYIA: An exploration by one of our Deep Submergence Rescue Vehicles revealed underground caverns smack dab in the middle of the Bermuda Triangle. For three years we searched, but found nothing. One day we found a dry cavern that seemed to be dug out.

SENAR: By whom?

SHELIA: Well, what we found was a badly damaged alien craft and a being in a cryogenic state. The being was retrieved and brought back to the lab.

ANYIA: It took three months for it to regain consciousness and two years to communicate. We discovered that the being was the last of its kind.

SENAR: Great! I thought you just came for the cookout. Now I'm in the middle of something I don't understand, even if I wasn't tipsy?

SHELIA: Before the creature or being passed on, it said, "One man's hope can save the universe! One man's faith can save us all." It also said, "They have been watching us for two hundred years" and how different life forms which have invaded the earth have been systematically purging the earth of us.

ANYIA: We also found out that the power this being had was tremendous. It could have destroyed us, but it chose to warn us.

SENAR: All of this is hard to swallow, but it would explain a lot of what I've seen, so now what do we do about it?

SHELIA: The only thing that can save us now is in the canister.

ANYIA: That's what she thinks.

SENAR: Come again.

SHELIA: The natural genetic make-up of this being releases spores that act as an antibody. The toxins tested from the first being that died were sent to a military lab, but it was her father that made the break through after several failures.

ANYIA: A toxin was created, and if magnified and released into the air, not only will it kill every virus known to man, but it will kill every non-human, non-mammal, and non-sea creature, so that is what's in the can, but that's only a small part. The fun will start soon after.

SHELIA: Since we were kids, Anyia has always told me that science won't save the world.

ANYIA: Jesus will.

SENAR: I don't know Shelia; I think you might better take her a little bit more serious.

SHELIA: Why?

SENAR: I'm not any rocket scientist like you, but uh there's something special about this girl. I do have one more question.

SHELIA: What's that?

SENAR: What about roaches?

SHELIA: Even insects would be gone.

SENAR: No more roaches?

ANYIA: Yes, Senar.

SENAR: Wow!

V.O. - Now having all the answers, Senar wished he never knew at all.

SHELIA: We must gather all the weapons, secure all the doors, and pray that we can survive the hours to develop the toxin.

ANYIA: Should we warn people or keep this to ourselves?

SENAR: I think people would rather die with a gun in their hands than to be ambushed in their day-to-day life.

ANYIA: I agree. I suggest that we bypass all the world news stations by satellite.

SHELIA: I'll get right on it.

Chapter Four
"Deep Secrets"

INT. SUB LEVEL 3. NIGHT

V.O. – As if on cue, all the power went out. Thirty seconds later emergency power kicked in. By now three of the seven entry points had been breached. Weapons were immediately distributed among all employees. High tech and conventional weapons were passed out. Sheila and all of us went three levels down below and began to work on the toxin. Her assistant, Maggie Waters, an Italian American athletic woman kept us posted on the integrity of our security. Their security force was fighting a good fight, but losing the battle slowly.

MAGGIE: I really think someone should use the tunnel to get the disc of the recorded warning to the public.

SENAR: Good idea, but who?

ANYIA: How far is the media center from here?

MAGGIE: About forty minutes.

ANYIA: Senar, can you still shoot with your left hand, being that your right shoulder is wounded?

SENAR: I'm ambidextrous.

MAGGIE: Level one just went down, so I guess I will have to take the disc myself.

V.O. Room gets quiet.

ANYIA: I'll go with you. You can't do this alone.

SENAR: I guess I'm going too!

MAGGIE: Level two has a very secure force field, so maybe we should eat and get some rest.

SHELIA: Yes, we have a heck of a task in front of us. I think it's a good idea.

SENAR: What's on the menu?

MAGGIE: You'll see soon enough.

ANYIA: I bet he will.

INT. WHITE HOUSE. NIGHT

V.0. – Meanwhile at the Pentagon and at the White House, panic had set in, not knowing whether to secretly try to evacuate this threat or to declare a state of emergency. Realizing there are too many trying to keep quiet, they decided to have a world leader conference call via satellite.

PRES. CLAYTON: I'm open to all suggestions, but first I would like to hear what our cabinet has to say before I speak to the other leaders.

V.P. POOL: Personally, I think it's too late to keep it quiet, so why not alert the public!

SEC. OF DEF. CHOI: It might cause mass hysteria.

CAPT. STOWE: I think that the canister is our only hope, and the only way to retrieve the canister is to become allies with those who have it.

PRES. CLAYTON: I agree. So the longer we take to get this canister, the death count worldwide will mount.

V.P. POOL: I'm afraid so, Mr. President.

CAPT. STOWE: I'll have my team ready and briefed within the hour.

SEC. OF DEF. CHOI: Very good. Please report to us as soon as this canister is found.

CAPT. STOWE: Yes, Sir.

EXT. STREETS. NIGHT

Pres. Clayton: Stowe I need a word with you in private.

Capt. Stowe: Yes Sir.

V.O. – Pres. Clayton and Capt. Stowe go into the oval office and close the door.

Capt. Stowe: How can I help you Sir?

Pres. Clayton: I've gotten a message from the Pope and in his message he wants us to take delivery of a package.

Capt. Stowe: What kind of package Sir?

Pres. Clayton: A pregnant nun.

Capt. Stowe: You got to be kidding me.

Pres. Clayton: No, I'm not kidding and I'm just giving this mission to you. Here are your orders.

Capt. Stowe: What you want us to do with them?

Pres. Clayton: Take her to area 51. They'll know what to do with her.

Capt. Stowe: Yes Sir.

V.O. – Meanwhile…On the streets of the world, death was mounting by the thousands.

"After this I looked and behold, a door was opened in heaven, and the first voice which I heard was as it were of a trumpet talking with me which said, Come hither, and I will shew you these things which must be hereafter."

Revelation 4:1

EXT. NEVADA DESERT. NIGHT

V.O. – Elsewhere…A Nevada couple driving home from the casino via the desert sees a crowd not far ahead.

DAVID: Pass me a beer, Emily.

EMILY: Don't you think you had enough?

DAVID: Not as long as there's some left.

EMILY: What am I going to do with you?

DAVID: Love me for eternity.

EMILY: That's a long time.

DAVID: We got time, my dear.

EMILY: Don't count on it, David, not if you keep drinking like you do.

V.O. – As they get closer to the crowd, what is in front of them begins to come clear. At first it looks like a costume party. Moments after getting too close to turn back, they didn't realize they were in the midst of 200 of the most deadly cross species ever created. What they saw was three overturned tour buses. Among the buses were mutilated bodies all over the highway. Bears and lions had been crossed with reptiles. Crosses of any deadly creatures and everything known to man had been made, but now there was competition. The aliens were at war and now it seems that the war in heaven is on its way to earth. Mr. and Mrs. David Davis saw they had no route for escape. She began to clutch her cross. Seconds later they were viciously mutilated. She died holding her left ring finger in her right hand. They had gotten remarried for the third time just the day before.

Chapter Five
"Man Playing God"

INT. SLEEPING QUARTERS. NIGHT

Senar V.O. – Meanwhile…back at the lab, Maggie Waters leads us to our rooms. Little did I know that I would be having company? As Maggie went in the room to put the linen out, Anyia stopped me.

ANYIA: Senar, everything ain't always what it seems.

SENAR: What do you mean?

ANYIA: Who do you see me as and what do you see me as?

SENAR: Okay, there you go scaring me again.

ANYIA: It's been a long day. Get some rest. I'll check in on you later.

SENAR: Is that a promise?

ANYIA: You bet your life on it.

SENAR V.O. – As I headed directly to the shower with the thoughts of Anyia stopping by later running through my mind, I couldn't help but think that maybe I'm really falling for this chick or was it some type of spiritual connection. I wasn't sure yet. Her spirit seems so familiar as though I met her before.

SENAR: Wow! Here I go again.

V.O. – Maggie decides to show Anyia her sleeping quarters. While in route, she had a few questions for her.

MAGGIE: So how long have you known Senar?

ANYIA: Not long at all.

MAGGIE: Y'all awfully close to have just met.

ANYIA: I know that's the strange thing.

MAGGIE: Come again.

ANYIA: My soul feels as though I've known him all my life, like we've met before.

MAGGIE: (Shoving the towels into her chest). This is your room right here. I hope you enjoy it.

ANYIA: I'm sure I will.

EXT. WOODS WEST VIRGINIA. NIGHT

V.O. - Meanwhile out in the woods, a group of soldiers walk toward the light that they see. Lead by Capt. Stowe, they push on advancing cautiously.

MCCOY: Why is the captain acting so funny?

CHET: I've been wondering that myself, and I intend to find out.

STEVENS: Sir, we've got fifteen men pulling up the flank, and the captain is leading. How come it seems like he knows where he's going?

CHET: You and McCoy hold back and wait for my word.

V.O. - Capt. Stowe advances to the middle of the field where the bright lights are. Someone greets him. He orders the rest of the men to lay down their weapons. Reluctantly they do so. Chet catches up to Capt. Stowe.

CHET: Sir, what are you doing?

CAPT. STOWE: I don't think you have the need to know clearance for this.

CHET: The hell I don't.

Capt. Stowe: Soldier, stay in your place.

Chet: My place is wherever my country sends me Sir.

Capt. Stowe: I've got a very important delivery to take here, so find somewhere else to play hero.

Chet: What kind of delivery Sir?

Capt. Stowe: He's here.

Chet: Who's here?

Capt. Stowe: You'll see soon.

V.O. – As Capt. Stowe goes over to the chopper, he escorts a woman out of it draped in an all black garment and helps her into the Hummer and tells the driver to stop at nothing and to defend her with his life. The soldier speeds away with security in tow. Stowe walks back over to Chet.

Capt. Stowe: Well I gotta go.

Chet: With all that security, you would think that you got the Pope in there.

Capt. Stowe: Close to it.

Chet: What do you mean?

Capt. Stowe: Let's just say you already know too much.

Chet: So Capt., tell me, how is Diane?

CAPT. STOWE: What?

CHET: Your wife, Sir.

CAPT. STOWE: She's fine, soldier. Thanks for asking.

V.O. - Chet gets on the radio and tells Stevens and McCoy to come to where he is immediately. He then orders the rest of the soldiers to pick up their weapons. As they are picking up their weapons, Capt. Stowe yells out.

CAPT. STOWE: What the hell are you doing, Chet?

CHET: I'm assuming command, Sir.

CAPT. STOWE: You're way out of your league.

CHET: No, Sir, actually I think you're about to be.

CAPT. STOWE: I don't get it.

CHET: Well, let me give it to you.

V.O. - Chet and the faithful few of his men draw on Capt. Stowe and his loyal soldiers.

CHET: I'm going to give the rest of you guys the chance that Capt. Stowe is not going to have. You see, Capt. Stowe doesn't have a wife any more. She died in the same car accident that killed my wife, so obviously you're not feeling yourself today, Sir.

V.O. - Immediately Capt. Stowe changes into his alien form. Chet pulls the trigger and blows him away. Those that were loyal to Stowe laid their guns down, and one by one Chet questioned them. All of them failed the test but one, so he shot them all. He begins to question the remaining soldier.

CHET: So, Erickson, you've known me for a while. Me being a Yankee fan, what do I hate most, more than a Red Sox fan and don't get it wrong.

ERICKSON: You got to be freaking joking, right?

CHET: Does it look like I'm laughing?

ERICKSON: You should be able to know me no matter what the freak is going on.

CHET: Just answer the freaking question.

ERICKSON: Two Red Sox fans.

CHET: Yeah, that's him. Move out.

Chapter Six
"More Than We Can Chew"

Day Three

INT. SLEEPING QUARTERS. SENAR'S ROOM. 1 AM

V.O. – Meanwhile Sheila knocks on Senar's door and asks if she can come in.

SHELIA: Well, I'm going to keep it real with you. We don't have as much time as I initially thought.

SENAR: How long are we talking?

SHELIA: Eleven hours at the most.

SENAR: Anybody else know this?

SHELIA: No, I wanted you to be the first because I have a few questions for you.

SENAR: Okay, I'll answer one. What is it?

SHELIA: Are you in love with Anyia?

SENAR: Okay, now you're tripping.

SHELIA: Oh no, not the king of keeping it real…going out like a sucker.

SENAR: (Defensively) Oh! You trying to play me, right?

SHELIA: (Attitude) No, I'm not trying to play you, but if you want to sit here and open up your big mouth and act like you are not in love with Anyia, you just played yourself.

SENAR: What I mean is…

SHELIA: Save it! Get some rest. I've got work to do…real work.

INT. SUB 3 CORRIDOR. 2 AM

V.O. – Meanwhile the integrity of the lab has totally fallen apart. Maggie Waters rushes up the hall to inform everybody that they have to go now! Anyia rushes down the hall to get

Senar. Maggie, Sheila, Anyia, and Senar rush toward the elevator leading to the tunnel. Fifteen other soldiers come out of their rooms. Everybody had a full metal jacket.

Senar V.O. - As I turned and looked down the hall, I could see that the beings had breached this floor. Soldiers were fighting for their lives, going down in a hail of bullets and teeth. I put Anyia behind me and I went to war too. As I backed towards the elevator, I draw both guns painfully and I began to fire at everything moving. Anyia drew both of her guns and wrapped her arms around my waist and began to fire also. It seemed like making it to the elevator took forever.

EXT. STREET. PRE DAWN

V.O. - Back in the city, there's carnage in the street. Marshall Law has been laid down. Beings from over three different planets are now battling each other for the right to herd us, while exterminating us down to a manageable number, but neither one of them was expecting the demonic forces that was to come.

V.O. – Meanwhile at Vatican City, the Pope is standing in front of the window talking to the Arch Bishop.

Arch Bishop: Do you realize what you have done?

Pope: I remember as though it was yesterday. The Virgin Mary came to me and told me what I must do.

Arch Bishop: We have gone to extreme measures to do this what you want of us.

Pope: Be patient. He is almost here now.

Arch Bishop: The 300 babies we killed in Florence, what was that for?

Pope: That was to hide all of the sexual infidelities that has plagued our church, but now what I have done, will bring it all out in the open.

Arch Bishop: Bring what?

Pope: You will soon see.

V.O. – Meanwhile back at the lab.

INT. ELEVATOR HALLWAY. PRE DAWN

V.O. - Senar, Anyia, Maggie, Sheila and Lu Choi make it to the elevator. Before the doors close, five more soldiers make it through. A sixth one makes it, but is yanked out the door by his head.

SENAR: Anybody hit?

SOLDIER 1: Yeah, my leg is messed up pretty bad.

ANYIA: I'm okay, I think I'm alright.

MAGGIE: Everything but my underwear is okay.

SHELIA: It's one thing to study them and to gather information on them, but watching them move and destroy like they do, I don't see how we have a chance. I should have done more field work. I should have been a doctor in a small town. I shouldn't be here.

MAGGIE: Get a freaking grip, alright, Sheila?

ANYIA: (Reaching over and hugging Sheila) Don't worry. I'm not going to let anything happen to you.

V.O. – Soldiers 2, 3, 4, and 5 agree to lead the charge once the elevator stops. Lu Choi decides he has something to say right before the elevator doors open.

LU CHOI: I have something I need to tell you all. What's in the canister is not going to kill the biggest threat that we are faced with.

V.O. – Just then the elevator doors open. They all take off running to the Suburban. The four soldiers, who said nothing, run up to the Suburban and open all the doors first. Just then they are all snatched into the truck and brutally ripped apart.

INT. EXIT TUNNEL. PRE DAWN

LU CHOI: Oh, my God! Did you see that? Guys, I really need to tell you something.

SENAR: What is it, man?

LU CHOI: That's what I've been meaning to tell you. Those are the ones that the toxins won't affect at all…the ones that just snatched them into the car. We haven't found anything to kill them yet, and they are the most vicious.

ANYIA: Let's go this way. I know where another car is.

MAGGIE: I'll cover the rear. Let's go!

SENAR: Anyia, stay behind me no matter what happens. Hold my belt and don't let go.

SHELIA: All my years of studying destroyed.

MAGGIE: You'd better come on or you're going to lose more than your work.

V.O. – They jump in the SUV and speed off down the tunnel.

Chapter Seven
"Remember When"

INT. CITY. PRE DAWN

V.O. – Back in the city a little girl is huddled up in the closet in an upstairs bedroom looking through a hole in the ceiling. She looks up at a star that she can see shining through, wishing her daddy was there, scared to death and hungry. She looks up at the stars and talks to the Lord. Looking up, she begins to say:

TOONIE: "Lord, I don't know what's going on, but if this is about me not cleaning my room, I'm sorry. I'll make sure I feed Sam every day, not once in a while. I'm sorry, but if I can ask you one more thing, Lord, please send my daddy to me."

EXT. WOODS. PRE DAWN

V.O. – Meanwhile at the edge of the woods, Lt. Chet rethinks his strategy.

CHET: We need to find the young lady that has the canister. I think they're the only ones we can trust right now. Ready the chopper.

STEVENS: Where are we going?

CHET: The big city baby.

EXT. SUV. INNER CITY. DAWN

V.O. – Meanwhile as Senar and his battered bunch speed down the highway towards the city, the truck is completely quiet. Anyia decides to break the silence.

ANYIA: I know it looks hopeless, but I promise if we don't give up, we will make it through this.

SENAR: Who's to say that the city is even open or running?

ANYIA: This is not about warning people any more. I'm pretty sure they already know. This is about getting this canister in the hands of the right people now. I just need to get to a working phone.

SHELIA: Who can we trust?

MAGGIE: Yeah, who can we trust?

LU CHOI: We can trust my father.

SOLDIER 1: Who's your father?

LU CHOI: Secretary of Defense Choi.

SHELIA: And here I thought I was getting funding because of my work. The whole time daddy's been funding you.

SENAR: I don't want to hear none of this right now. Let's just get to the city, find a phone and find my daughter.

EXT. INNER CITY. DAWN

V.O. – Meanwhile back in the desert a group of Black Op Commandos heading to area 51 with the strange woman sitting in the back seat covered in black; attempt to neutralize the escaped cross-breed problem with little success. Although they were slaughtered, the woman in the back seat walks off in the desert between the beast and not one dare to touch her. She sees a cave and walks to the very back to lie down and wait.

V.O. – Meanwhile back in the city.

SENAR V.O – Pulling into the city I could smell death all around us. For everybody that I saw, I could only imagine in what horrible way that they died, wondering how my baby could have survived this.

An army truck crosses in front of us, and warns us to stay out of the south street area. He said biological life forms had saturated the area. Today wasn't a good day for taking orders. I had to find my daughter.

V.O. – A jeep pulled up beside the truck.

SOLDIER 7: Turn around. You don't want to go through that area.

ANYIA: We have to.

SOLDIER 7: Well, if you do, don't say I didn't warn you.

SENAR: Okay, we'll keep that in mind.

V.O. – As they drive through the city slowly, Sheila starts to freak out.

SHELIA: Did you see the claw marks in that car door? What can do something like that?

MAGGIE: Something that had years to grow finger nails.

SENAR: Keep your eyes open. My daughter's house is right around the corner. Kill the lights.

EXT. TOONIE HOUSE. DAWN

V.O. – They roll up to the house slowly with the lights out.

SENAR: Give me the AK and the night vision. It's dark inside that house. I always wanted to wear one of these, but not under these circumstances.

ANYIA: Let's go.

SENAR: What do you mean, let's? You're staying here.

ANYIA: I thought it was you and me.

SENAR: That's my whole point. I got a funny feeling there's no me without you, so you stay here. Maggie, Lu Choi, Sheila, guard her with your life.

SENAR: (Talking to Soldier 1) You come with me.

INT. TOONIE HOUSE. DAWN

V.O. – As Senar walks through the front door slowly creeping his way in, he tells the soldier to stay at the door and watch his back. The soldier responds:

SOLDIER 1: Who's going to watch my back?

SENAR: The truck is right in front of the door. They got you.

V.O. – Senar gets to the staircase and looks up the steps, but just before he takes a step to walk up, he sees Toonie huddled up in a corner in the hall shaking in terror. Just by the look in her eyes, he knew something was wrong. He got down on one knee and reached his hand out gesturing to her to come to him. She shakes her head no, and then she looks up to her left and looks back at him. Senar, not knowing what's behind the wall, he can only imagine. Just then her mother Cookie steps up.

COOKIE: Hey, Senar. Long time no see. Come here; let me take a good look at you.

V.O. – Senar also begins to get very worried. She had never been this nice to him. She looks at Senar. She looks as hard as she can to the left and then back at him. With tears rolling down her face, he noticed she would not move her hands.

SENAR: What's wrong, Cookie? Send Toonie to me.

COOKIE: I can't do that, baby.

V.O. – Senar draws his gun and walks slowly toward Cookie. They look eye to eye. Sweat pouring down his face as he enters closer to her, he decides to go for all or nothing.

SENAR: You remember those high heel shoes I bought you for your birthday?

COOKIE: Yes.

SENAR: What did you always do every time you wore those shoes?

V.O. – Cookie laughs. She falls to the floor. Senar fires through the wall on her left hand side.

A loud screech screams as Cookie is thrown into the wall while pulling a tentacle from the back of her neck. The creature falls to the floor dead from behind the wall.

TOONIE: (Toonie yells out) Daddy! Daddy!

V.O. – She runs to him and jumps in his arms.

SENAR: Oh, baby, are you alright?

TOONIE: Yeah I'm alright. That thing stuck something in mommy's neck trying to trick you. She didn't mean to do it.

V.O. – Senar runs over and checks on Cookie. Soldier 1 runs through the back door.

SOLDIER 1: What is that on the floor?

SENAR: Never mind that. You got some smelling salts in your bag?

SOLDIER 1: No, sure don't.

V.O. – Senar pours water in her face.

SENAR: Wake up, Cookie, come on, wake up. We got to get out of here.

V.O. – Cookie opens up one eye.

COOKIE: (Dazed) You're still as ugly as you used to be.

TOONIE: Yeah, my mama must be alright. She's herself again.

SENAR: Yeah, being a witch again. Come on. Let's go. Let's get out of here.

V.O. – Senar picks Cookie up and carries her to the truck.

"And their dead bodies shall lie in the street of the great city, which spiritually is called Sodom and Egypt, where also our Lord was crucified."

Revelations 11:8

"And I saw an angel come down from heaven, having the key of the bottomless pit and a great chain in his hand."

"Revelations 20:1"

Chapter Eight
"Day Late Dollar Short"

EXT. INNER CITY. DAWN

V.O. – Meanwhile Chet and his crew are now in the city and they are looking for Anyia and Senar.

ERICKSON: You are the definition of a prick. You were gonna shoot me.

CHET: I had to be sure. It's a lot riding on us.

ERICKSON: Would you care to fill me in?

CHET: At first I thought we were being invaded by a few of our friends and a couple of their enemies, but I now believe it's bigger than we can even imagine.

STEVENS: What do you exactly mean, Sir?

MCCOY: The end of Days! Book of REVELATION! My mom use to read the Bible, but she never really liked to read that particular book.

ERICKSON: Why?

MCCOY: She said the ending was beautiful, but it's a horror film before then. She said Steven King ain't got nothing on this, the things that will happen before the Lord comes.

CHET: Well I guess we are living history as we speak.

STEVENS: Who's history?

MCCOY: Our own.

EXT. TRUCK. HIGHWAY. MORNING

V.O. – Senar and the other survivors speed away from the city with the sun reflecting in the rear view mirror, but as they turn and look back, the fire and the death that they leave behind saddens their hearts. They ride, not really knowing what the future holds.

ANYIA: All those people, all those souls.

SENAR: What you talking about, Anyia?

ANYIA: All those people who didn't know today would be their last day. All those people who didn't live today looking ahead to tomorrow. That's why I only live one day at a time boo; one hour, one minute, one breath.

SOLDIER 1: Now what are we going to do?

ANYIA: Fulfill our destiny.

MAGGIE: What destiny, girl? Can't you see life is almost over?

SHELIA: It might be over for you, but my destiny is waiting for me.

COOKIE: I want to know why she's always talking in riddles.

SENAR: Listen, we just need to find somewhere safe to get some rest till we get our thoughts together.

SOLDIER 1: Looks like there is a shed over there about a half a mile east.

TOONIE: Daddy, I keep having this dream an angel saying to me everything is going to be alright. The Lord is coming. We must prepare his way, and when she turned and walked away, she had a tattoo on the back of her neck that looked like a butterfly.

SENAR: (While hugging her tightly) I believe you baby, I believe you, baby.

V.O. - As Anyia looks at Senar and Toonie with a strange stare, she drops her head as if she has a secret. As they drive down the highway not knowing their fate, for the first time in his life, Senar knows that the Lord is really with him and he is filled with a sense of purpose.

EXT. FRONT OF HOSPITAL. MORNING

V.O. - Meanwhile in the inner city looking for Anyia. Chet and his men find their way to the hospital, but little did they know that the hospital was a hot zone.

ERICKSON: Sir, something about this just doesn't feel right.

STEVENS: Yea, I know what you mean. I'm getting that same feeling.

MCCOY: I wish you two mama's boys would stop whining and keep your eyes open.

CHET: Shh, hold up. Everybody down!

MCCOY: What is it, Lt.?

CHET: I think you should really think about saying a few prayers right about now.

ERICKSON: What do you mean, Sir?

CHET: Area 51 rejects.

V.O. – Stevens pulls out a picture of his wife and daughter. He looks at it and then gives it a kiss. Erickson looks up into the sky as the rest of the men realize that they're now surrounded by the cross species of area 51. They turn and face the beasts, and then they look at each other. They charged towards the beasts, guns blazing.

Chapter Nine
"What's The Plan?"

INT. WAR ROOM. MORNING

V.O. – Meanwhile back at the Pentagon, the President and his cabinet discuss ways of neutralizing the situation.

VP POOL: Sir, I think you and the United Nations should convene.

PRES.CLAYTON: What are we going to convene for? Every government in the world is in a state of panic.

SEC. OF DEF. CHOI: I think we can link up via satellite.

V.O. – Just then the door slams open. It's Secretary of State Carmen Rivera.

CARMEN: Here's the plan gentlemen. We're gonna get another team together. We're gonna go into the city and we're gonna find Lt. Chet and this girl with the canister. I'm pretty sure they should be needing backup by now. Disperse all military personnel that we have at our disposal into the city. We must take control of that area. That canister is priority 1 and that girl is priority 1b, so while ya'll sit here with ya'll thumbs in your butts still playing government, you have to actually have live people and a functioning nation to be considered a president.

VP POOL: (Sarcastically) Who you think you are? Where do you come off judging us of our handling of this situation? There's no protocol for things like this and I'm sorry I missed the freaking memo and if there is a memo I'm sorry I missed the freaking memo.

SEC. OF DEF. CHOI: Ms. Rivera seems to be on the ball, so my suggestion is that we let her push it up court.

PRES. CLAYTON: Ms. Rivera, you have my authority to use any means necessary to neutralize the situation. Good luck and God speed.

V.P. POOL: Sir, what are you doing?

PRES. CLAYTON: Can I talk to you for a moment, privately?

V.P. POOL: Yes Sir.

PRES. CLAYTON: I have something more important that I am trying to keep track of right now.

V.P. POOL: I understand your position Sir, but I don't really believe in that religious mumbo jumbo. I just deal with facts and the fact is that we haven't received one report from Stowe since he went out there to retrieve the package Sir.

PRES. CLAYTON: Because of the Pope's private financial support, I'm able to look in my daughter's face again.

V.P. POOL: She's not your daughter Sir.

PRES. CLAYTON: She comes from her DNA, so she's my daughter.

V.P. POOL: A clone is no different than a living picture of a person. It's just an image Sir.

PRES. CLAYTON: I will not discuss this with you here or now.

V.O. – Pres. Clayton walks out the room and slams the door.

SEC. OF DEFENSE CHOI: We haven't heard from Stowe or Chet. At the moment, communications are down. We are trying to get a link up now.

CARMEN: V.P. Pool, tell me I just didn't hear that?

V.P. POOL: Hear what?

CARMEN: How could the President's daughter still be alive?

V.P. POOL: Technically she's not, between me and you.

CARMEN: Where is she?

V.P. POOL: Hidden away, where only he can see her.

CARMEN: Oh my God and this man has been running our country. Why tell this now Pool?

V.P. POOL: Who's going to be around to report it anyway?

V.O. – Carmen walks out the room shaking her head.

"And when he had opened the seventh seal, there was silence in heaven about the space of half an hour. And I saw the seven angels which stood before God, and to them were given seven trumpets."

Revelation 8:1, 2

EXT. FARM. DAY

V.O. – Senar and the rest of the group sees an abandoned shed off the side of the road in a field. As Senar and Anyia ride down the road leading to the shed, the scene almost looked like a painting, wide opened fields outlined by giant trees and the sun shining brightly above them. They all get out of the SUV and stood around, pondering what could await them inside.

SENAR: Soldier what's your name?

SOLDIER 1: Dean Sir, my name is Dean.

SENAR: Ok Dean, me, you and Anyia are going to check the shed out. The rest of you stay here and keep your eyes open. Shelia here, take my A.K. and Maggie if there is something wrong give us two shots in the air.

MAGGIE: If I shoot twice it's not going to be in the air.

V.O. - Senar and the gang check out the shed and confirm that it is abandoned. No signs of life whatsoever. They gather up what food and water they can find and settle in to catch their breath. We make it in without incident, but as we all know peace never lasts long.

SENAR V.O. - I remember when I was a little boy and I used to play in the strangest of places. My mind would take me anywhere. Some of the things that I would imagine would somewhere later on in life manifest itself for real. I'll never forget that one night when the house was real quiet and my sister was sleep in the bed across from me. Hearing footsteps from the hall that I can see from my bed, I sat up and saw nothing. This happened about four to five times. I finally got up and tried to wake my sister because usually when I lift up, the footsteps would stop, but this time they just kept coming. My sister slept with her eyes open; even then she couldn't see the terror on my face. As the footsteps got louder, I turned to run back to my bed, but something stood in front of me. It was about eight feet tall with a black hat and wearing a full length black trench coat. It had no features in its face, for its face was forever changing. I tried to run, but I couldn't move. I tried to scream, but nothing came out. I remember it picked me up, laid me on my bed and sat on my chest. I could feel the tears run down the side of my face and then I remembered what my mama told me. She said, there's power in the name of Jesus, but that's another story. We checked the barn and the barn was all clear. Me, Anyia and Toonie laid together on some hay looking through the hole in the roof. Man, it was so peaceful. Like with anything, nothing stays the same for long.

INT. SHED. DUSK

MAGGIE: So Cookie are you alright?

COOKIE: Yeah I'm fine. It could have been a lot worse.

SHELIA: Can I take a look at that wound on the back of your neck? Wow that looks bad. I think these creatures had some type of live bacteria on them. It looks like the flesh eating kind.

MAGGIE: So what does that mean?

COOKIE: Yeah, what does that mean?

SHELIA: You're gonna need help fast or that bacteria will eat right through you.

SENAR: We need to make it to the hospital. It's just a little east of here.

EXT. IN THE FIELD. SUN SET

SENAR V.O. – Me and Anyia decided to take a walk in the field. I grabbed some flowers off the ground as we walked along and watched the sun set. The look in her eyes was one of sheer peace.

ANYIA: Senar if I told you something would you believe me?

SENAR: About right now I'll believe anything.

ANYIA: What if you knew you were different, but couldn't tell anybody?

SENAR: It depends on how different I am and it would depend on whether the difference was good or bad.

ANYIA: What if you could give up your life to save the world? Would you want that choice? Would you really want it?

SENAR: Me myself, I would want it because my life never been really worth nothing and at least then I'd feel like my life had some sort of purpose.

ANYIA: What if I told you that you being here is no coincidence? What if I told you that one day you might have to make that choice and what if I told you that you are one of seven people who would be given that choice?

SENAR: I would say you are full of crap, with all due respect.

ANYIA: So that means you lied when you said you believe me.

SENAR: You're right. My bad, so you're saying that a piece of crap like me would play an important part in something that important. Yes, I do find that hard to believe.

ANYIA: What if I told you that it was our destiny to make love. Would you believe that?

SENAR: (Laughing out loud) Hell yeah! I think I had that dream myself.

ANYIA: That's funny?

SENAR: (Surprised) Word! You really want to make love to me?

ANYIA: No, I was just making a point.

V.O. – He leans over to kiss her and she pushes him to the ground.

ANYIA: No Senar, this cannot happen. To give into the flesh will only weaken our spirit and right now we need to be strong.

SENAR: Ok, I must have gotten the wrong signal.

ANYIA: Yeah, you must have. Long ago I came to you and told you I would be here.

SENAR: What are you talking about? Wait a minute, nah ain't no way.

V.O. – She walks away staring into Senar's eyes as he follows.

SENAR: How is that even possible?

ANYIA: All souls know each other. It's the flesh that is the stranger.

SENAR: So what is it that's drawing everybody together?

ANYIA: God's will.

SENAR: What do you know about that demon that visited me when I was seven years old?

ANYIA: The evil one always tries to devour those of us with a gift, given to us by the Holy Spirit to do God's will.

SENAR: So what's my purpose Anyia?

ANYIA: Only God knows that, but I do know that you are a gatekeeper.

SENAR: A what?

ANYIA: Your soul is one of protection and faith.

SENAR: What's yours?

ANYIA: One of sacrifice, love and hope.

SENAR: It's a beautiful sky tonight. I always wondered what it would be like if I had never seen the stars before because when I'm dead and gone I won't remember seeing them anyway.

ANYIA: You won't have to remember, one day we will walk among the stars.

Chapter Ten
"Leave No One Behind"

INT. PENTAGON. NIGHT

V.O. – Meanwhile back at the Pentagon Carmen Rivera gets a message on a covert network that Lt. Chet had requested immediate backup. He goes on to say...

Chet's covert message: Stowe wasn't who we thought he was. Don't know which planet. They transported a girl, don't know from where or where to. Trust no one.

V.O. – She then brings this to the attention of Secretary of Defense Lu Choi.

CARMEN RIVERA: Sit down! Look, Can I talk to you off the record?

LU CHOI: You mean we can actually do that.

CARMEN: What do you know about a package that Stowe was supposed to pick up?

LU CHOI: That's highly sensitive.

CARMEN: Don't play politics with me right now Lu Choi.

LU CHOI: Honestly, you wouldn't believe me if I told you.

CARMEN: Try me.

LU CHOI: For years the Vatican has been funding a lot of our black op projects in exchange for us turning a blind eye to some information that stumbled literally into our hands.

CARMEN: What do you mean?

LU CHOI: A girl escaped from the Vatican a few years back with video tapes and pictures of girls who have been kidnapped from all over the world. They were being held in a prison in Vatican City.

CARMEN: Kidnapped, for what?

LU CHOI: A lot of the girls were kidnapped from Brazil and some were actually bought from the parents.

CARMEN: Oh my God! My mother sent my sister away with some nuns from the church. Oh Lord!

LU CHOI: These girls were used for sexual orgies involving the monks to the Pope.

CARMEN: You got to be kidding me.

LU CHOI: Skeletons of babies have been found in tombs all around Vatican City from the babies that were discarded by the priests to keep up the image of the church.

CARMEN: What about this girl?

LU CHOI: We took her in, cleaned her up, interrogated her and put her in a safe house not even the President has access to.

CARMEN: So in other words she's being used for leverage.

LU CHOI: It works out for everybody. We get the money, we keep our mouths shut and they can keep on being perverts, rapist and murderers.

CARMEN: What else did the girl say?

LU CHOI: That the Virgin Mary supposedly appeared to the Pope and told him to be with the Brazilian woman whom they had captured and their seed should be special.

CARMEN: Special how, that can't be good?

LU CHOI: Can you say Antichrist?

CARMEN: Do you know how crazy this all sounds?

LU CHOI: What is crazy anymore?

CARMEN RIVERA: When I was a little girl growing up in Brazil, we used to see a lot of things, and my grandma used to say that the jungle holds many secrets, and there is this one particular place that she took me to when I was a little girl, and she said this is where the magic people live. One day she took me to this cave and in this cave there were writings on the wall and pictures and hieroglyphics (ancient drawings) on the walls.

LU CHOI: Why do you bring this up now?

CARMEN RIVERA: This girl Anyia, fit's a story of an ancient prophecy that was told of in the cave.

LU CHOI: You can't be serious. Are you?

CARMEN RIVERA: I know I know. It sounds crazy coming out of my mouth, but at the same time did you believe last week you would be seeing some of the things that you are dealing with now.

LU CHOI: Once again you've got a good point, so let's say that what you are saying has any truth to it. How does that tie in to what we are dealing with now?

CARMEN RIVERA: A legend has it that this girl supposedly is the modern day John the Baptist.

LU CHOI: Come again.

CARMEN RIVERA: Well Ok. Remember, keep an open mind to what I am about to tell you.

LU CHOI: Yeah just give it to me raw.

CARMEN RIVERA: Well.

V.O. - Just then Pres. Clayton and Vice Pres. Pool explode into the room.

V.P. POOL: We have a problem.

PRES. CLAYTON: That's a minor understatement.

SENAR V.O. (flashback from rooftop) - It's getting harder to breathe now. Harder to concentrate, but for some reason my mind is playing like in a movie. I remember leaving the shed with everyone all packed up with a look of lost hope on their faces. As much as I wanted to give up myself, I couldn't let anyone see it. I felt like everyone was relying on me for some reason, but I felt that I had the strength only to carry myself, so I prayed to God to help me carry the rest. We made it to the hospital, but never did I realize that our time in life as we know it was about to begin to come to an end.

EXT. HOSPITAL. NIGHT

V.O. - As Senar leaves the truck, first he hears nothing but silence and the rest of the crew falls out behind him.

SENAR: Dean, Anyia come with me. Everybody else form a perimeter around the truck. Guard it with your life.

ANYIA: I can sense something very powerful and very evil.

DEAN: I can smell the death in the air.

Senar V.O. - Just like those days when I was small and I just watched a scary movie, the hairs on the back of my neck stood up and the wind began to stand still and time began to slow down. Whatever that was about to happen was to begin now.

ANYIA: What's that? Something moved over there.

SENAR: Shh! Get down.

V.O. - Just then something snatches Dean up in the air and split him down the middle from head to toe, blood flies everywhere. Anyia begins to scream. As Senar and Anyia run for their lives, Senar grabs Anyia and throws her over his shoulder while firing; clearing a path in front of them. They are being attacked by the area 51-200. Senar and Anyia run through the doorway and through a long corridor. As they look behind them, they seem to be temporarily safe. Senar stops and gets on the radio.

INT. FREEZER. NIGHT

SENAR: (Talking on two-way) Maggie- Senar, come in.

MAGGIE: Maggie- go ahead.

SENAR: Leave the area immediately. Get out of there now; go back to the shed, that's an order.

ANYIA: Senar wait, I hear something.

SENAR: It's coming from inside that freezer.

ANYIA: Whatever it is, it's hurt badly.

V.O. - As Senar opens the door to the freezer a badly mangled Chet falls out the door. As Anyia stands there speechless and stunned, Senar catches Chet before he hits the ground.

CHET: (In a very weak voice) They're all dead. They're all dead.

SENAR V.O. - As I look around the freezer, I see the rest of his crew hanging on hooks. Chet had managed to wiggle himself off of his. Me and Anyia grabbed Chet and ran toward the emergency room. I knew I could find a vehicle there.

V.O. - Meanwhile Shelia, Maggie and the rest of the crew raced back to the shed to grab ammo and grenades.

EXT. HIGHWAY. NIGHT

TOONIE: Is my daddy alright? Are they going to be ok?

SHELIA: They're going to be fine.

MAGGIE: Yeah, they're going to be fine because we're going back to get them. I don't think Senar or Anyia would have left us.

COOKIE: Why we going back, he said go to the shed.

CHOI: You wouldn't be sitting here if he hadn't saved your ungrateful butt.

MAGGIE: Enough of this reality show crap. Let's go back to the shed and get some more ammo and grenades.

CHOI: Ok, here we go.

V.O. - Choi, Maggie, Shelia, Toonie, and Cookie set their plans in motion to try and find Senar and Anyia. They looked around the shed to see if they could find anything at all that would help them conquer these creatures. Out in the back they found more ammo. They all loaded their guns and hopped into the truck.

INT. EMERGENCY ROOM. NIGHT

V.O. – Meanwhile Senar and Anyia are searching desperately for a vehicle to get the hell out of there. On the way down the long corridor they come across their worst nightmare.

SENAR: You got to be joking right. Anyia stay close by me.

CHET: Alright. It's between you and it and it better be you.

ANYIA: Senar I got this, just help Chet and find that vehicle. I am tired of these things already.

SENAR: I can't let you do this by yourself. You are gonna need my help.

ANYIA: Go, I'll holler if I need you.

V.O. – Anyia looked the creature squarely in the eyes and said bring it on. The creature proceeded closer to Anyia, while Anyia drew her gun that she got from Chet. Blazing her gun and throwing knives that she retrieved from another dead soldier, she gave it everything she had. Senar slid past Anyia carrying Chet over his shoulder while agonizing over the pain in his other shoulder. They found a vehicle backed on the side of the hospital. Senar put Chet inside while he went back for Anyia. The battle was hard, but Anyia wasn't backing down. The creature sliced her arm with his claws. Angry now, Anyia slid under him and shot the back of his head. Anyia turned around and saw Senar coming back for her.

SENAR: Anyia, you alright? Let's get out of here.

ANYIA: Where's Chet?

SENAR: I located a vehicle and he is waiting for us.

ANYIA: Senar, thanks for coming back for me.

SENAR: You would have done the same for me. Come on let's take care of that wound on your arm.

ANYIA: I'm ok, let's get to the shed and make sure the others are safe.

"And I will give power unto my two witnesses and they shall prophecy a thousand two hundred and three score days clothed in sack cloth. These are the two olive trees and the two candle sticks standing before the God of the earth."

Revelation 11:3, 4

"And if any man will hurt them fire proceeded out of their mouth and devour their enemies and if any man will hurt them he must in this manner be killed."

Revelation 11:5

Chapter Eleven
"Is Anybody Out There?"

DAY FOUR

EXT. HIGHWAY. PRE DAWN

V.O. – Exhausted and wounded Anyia, Senar, and Chet head towards the shed seeing headlights headed directly at them. They pull over to flag the vehicle down. Longing for any kind of human contact besides their own, they're hoping someone else has some answers. As the vehicle pulls over, Anyia is happy to see that it is the rest of the gang from the shed. They gather on the side of the road discussing what to do next. Senar suggests they leave the area because of the threat that's all around them. Senar had a few questions for Chet.

SENAR: What were ya'll doing out here?

CHET: I was acting on a hunch and it paid off. My captain was one of those aliens and we caught him transporting some woman in a top secret convoy.

SENAR: Who was she?

CHET: There's no telling, it was totally black ops, but I do know she had the Vatican symbol on her garment.

SENAR: We'll talk later because I still don't know what's going on.

CHET: What's your story?

SENAR: It's a long one.

CHET: Who's the chick? Is this the one Carmen made a big deal about?

SENAR: Who's Carmen?

CHET: She's been looking for you guys.

SENAR: Why?

CHET: That freaking canister.

SENAR: Give me the canister Anyia. I'll take that burden off your shoulders.

ANYIA: It's not a burden, it's an honor.

SENAR: (Taking the canister out of her backpack and putting it into his) Well let's share the glory.

SHELIA: I think it's time to head south. Make it to the Pentagon.

LU CHOI: Yeah, I need to convene with my father. I can get us access to the equipment that we need in order to complete the process.

MAGGIE: Let's say we get it to the Pentagon. Do you know how to synthesize and magnify the spores?

SENAR: How do we disperse them?

SHELIA: That's why we need to get to the Pentagon. They have all the toys that we need.

TOONIE: Did somebody say toys?

COOKIE: Not those kind of toys I'm sure.

SENAR V.O. – I remember that trip so well. I remember how hopeless I felt at that time, but something about the look in Anyia's eyes gave me hope. Halfway down the road we begin to see how far the devastation had spread. The moon shines brightly and lights up the road as I drive down I-95 with Toonie sleeping up against me and Anyia sleeping up against her. I find myself to be the only one awake. As each hour passed by, the things I saw began to soften my soul and reminded me of how great my life was no matter how bad, before now.

V.O.– As the two vehicles head south down I-95, Senar, Toonie, Anyia, Cookie, and Maggie are in the first vehicle and Chet, Lu Choi and Shelia are in the second vehicle. Both vehicles speed down the highway not knowing what awaits them.

SENAR: Anyia wake up.

ANYIA: Why?

SENAR: I see lights up ahead in that building.

ANYIA: Ok wake me up when we get there.

SENAR: No wake up I'm serious.

ANYIA: Ok Senar I'm awake now. I'm sorry I was just so tired.

MAGGIE: Did somebody say lights?

SENAR: Good you woke. Everybody get ready for the unexpected.

MAGGIE: That's no problem. I always expect the unexpected.

ANYIA: Maybe somebody else is alive.

SENAR: What makes you think that?

ANYIA: I don't know I just feel it.

SENAR: Wake up Cookie. We need everybody alert.

Chapter Twelve
"The Cows Ain't What They Seem"

EXT. OUTSIDE BAR. DAWN

V.O. - As Senar pulls up to the abandoned bar, Chet pulls up behind him. They all get out with their guns cocked. Senar tells Toonie and Cookie to get in the truck with Chet, Shelia, and Lu Choi.

SENAR: Y'all stay here with Chet. Me, Anyia and Maggie are going inside to see what's up.

CHET: Why we stopping here anyway?

ANYIA: It might be something in there we can use.

MAGGIE: Yeah, I could use a drink anyway.

SENAR: Come on let's go.

INT. BAR. DAWN

V.O. - Senar, Maggie and Anyia walk through the door of the bar. Bodies and blood are everywhere. Anyia can't help but shed a tear for the souls that lie there dead.

MAGGIE: What the hell came through here?

ANYIA: I don't know, but I hope it's gone.

V.0. - Just then Senar hears a loud bang and what sounds like screaming.

SENAR: Did you hear that?

MAGGIE: Hear what?

V.O. - Just then there's a loud bang and a scream again.

SENAR: That!

ANYIA: Sounds like it's coming from back there.

SENAR: Anyia, stay behind me. Maggie, watch our back. Let's go!

V.O. – As Senar and Anyia approach the door, the banging gets

louder. Anyia and Maggie position themselves on each side of the door. Senar stands in front of the door and then kicks the door open. Just when he's about to pull the trigger, voices scream out "Don't Shoot." Two lone surviving bartenders scream out for their life.

SENAR: Who are you?

KYLA: (Screaming out loud) I'm Kyla, this is Renee. Please don't kill us.

MAGGIE: Are you here alone?

RENEE: Yeah it's just us.

KYLA: Who are you?

SENAR: Give me one good reason why we should believe you?

Anyia: That's a good point.

MAGGIE: Let's just shoot them to be sure.

RENEE: No wait, here, look in my purse. I have pictures of me and my kids.

MAGGIE: Wrong answer, let's just shoot them.

ANYIA: Wait Maggie, I know how to find out. Pull your sleeve up.

KYLA: What?

MAGGIE: Pull your sleeve up.

SENAR: We insist.

V.O. – Senar and Maggie hold Kyla's arms from both sides. Anyia rolls up her sleeves, pulls out a pocket knife and cuts her. Kyla yells out, "What the heck? Oh no, let me go."

SENAR: Is she good?

ANYIA: Yeah she's good. That's human.

KYLA: What?

MAGGIE: Ok, Renee you're up.

RENEE: This is ridiculous, she don't have to cut me.

MAGGIE: I could just shoot you instead.

V.O. – Senar and Maggie hold Renee while Anyia pulls out the pocket knife. Just then Lu Choi runs through the door. "Guys we got to go, we got company." Just then Anyia cuts Renee across the forearm.

Renee turns and looks at Senar and smiles; then she throws Senar and Maggie 20 feet each way. Anyia jumps out of the way as Renee runs toward the door turning into her alien form. She literally runs through Lu Choi, killing him instantly. Just then you hear a burst of gunfire and then silence. Chet runs through the door. "Are y'all alright?" Come on lets go. We have to get out of here.

SENAR: Lu Choi is he.

CHET: Dead, yes and if you don't want to be, you'll move your butt now. Remember your daughter is in the car.

EXT. OUTSIDE BAR. SUNRISE

V.O. - As Maggie, Anyia and Senar gather themselves and follow Chet back to the SUV they almost forgot they had another passenger running behind them, Kyla yells out.

KYLA: Don't leave me; I didn't know she was an alien.

MAGGIE: Well you better run like you stole something, because here they come.

V.O. - They run back to the SUV's and speed off south going down I-95 headed to the Pentagon.

INT. PENTAGON. MORNING

V.O. - Early morning back at the Pentagon.

PRES. CLAYTON: Mr. Pool have you heard anything from Chet's command?

V.P. POOL: No I haven't sir. I am waiting on word now.

SEC. OF DEF. CHOI: Has there been any word on the location of this canister that we need to have?

CARMEN RIVERA: I'm waiting on confirmation on that also.

V.O. - A soldier opens the door and hands Ms. Rivera a note and leaves.

CARMEN RIVERA: I'm afraid I have some bad news Sir. One of our area patrols found Lt. Chet's unit mutilated in a hospital on the edge of the kill zone. Everybody's tags had been recovered except for Lt. Chet's. Somehow he managed to survive, I'm assuming or at least got away from that particular area.

PRES. CLAYTON: The whole unit?

CARMEN RIVERA: I'm afraid so Sir.

LU CHOI: What about the canister?

CARMEN: A small patrol has seen some survivors that fit their description not more than 60 miles from where Lt Chet's men were massacred.

V.P. POOL: You think they might have met up somehow, someway?

CARMEN: I hope so, I really hope so.

"And when I saw him I fell at his feet as dead. And he laid his right hand upon me saying unto me, fear not I am the first and the last I am he that liveth and was dead and behold I am alive ever more, Amen and have the keys of hell and of death."

Revelation 1:17

EXT. EDGE OF BEACH. MORNING

V.O. - In the Channel Islands on the island of San Miguel, a woman known as Sarah Catherine walks through the brush down to the beach with her three grandchildren, Dena, Michael and Rachel. As they get to the bottom of the brush, she sees something fly past her, but she's not sure what it was. Sarah has long been rumored to be sort of an unspoken spiritual visionary. Legend has it that as a baby she was left on a rock in the middle of the river where she stayed for seven days and seven nights. Her mother truly believed that the Lord had touched her and sent her here for a reason. She also believed that the Angels would watch over her. At the time, there was civil unrest in their village because something had made all the men go mad. They were killing all the women and children looking for something that they never found. Soon after, all the men were either killed by authority or went mad and killed themselves. Sarah was the lone survivor. Sarah Catherine gets to the bottom of the brush and sits on a rock across from a log that her three grandchildren sit on.

DENA: Grandmamma, what was it like when you was a little girl?

SARAH: Oh baby I was just like you.

RACHEL: What about me?

SARAH: I was like you too.

MICHAEL: I know you wasn't like me; cause I'm a boy.

SARAH: Oh yeah I was! I climbed trees, threw rocks, and could swim across a river.

DENA: I told you Michael.

MICHAEL: What?

DENA: You ain't the first boy whose sister could beat him in everything.

RACHEL: (Laughing) Yeah I'm sure there's a long list of losers just

like you.

SARAH: Ok kids let me tell y'all a story.

V.O. - Just then a 20 foot white anaconda lowers himself from a tree above her grandchildren. Trying not to panic the children, she continues to tell the story. The children, not being aware of the threat above them, are focused and hanging on every word their grandmamma said.

Sarah then turns to the children and tells them "I need you to take a nap now. I need to talk to someone." She waves her hand from right to left and all three children fall asleep on the grass. She turns to the snake and says, "Why are you here."

SNAKE: Ssstories are my favorite.

SARAH: Enjoy your time because your end is soon.

SNAKE: Sssarah, Sssarah, Sssarah. Watch thy tongue before I smite thy children.

SARAH: My God and my Lord Jesus will not let you harm me nor my seeds, so go back hither where you come from.

SNAKE: We shall sssee.

V.O.– Just then the snake leaped down to pounce on the children, but just before he reached them a lightning bolt from the sky shot down from the heavens and blew the snake apart. Sarah got on her knees and said….

SARAH: Thank you Jesus O Father thou art in heaven hallowed be thy name thy kingdom come thou will be done on earth as it is in heaven forgive us for our trespasses as we forgive those who have trespassed against us, lead us not into temptation but deliver us from evil. For thine is the kingdom the power and the glory forever and ever Amen. Wake up children….

V.O. – The children wake up and find themselves lying on the ground. They are confused, but not afraid.

MICHAEL: How did we get on the ground?

RACHEL: Yuck, what's this all over us?

DENA: I don't know, but I had a dream grandma blew up a snake.

V.O. – As Rachel turned to get up, she sees the snake head lying behind her. She turns and looks at her grandmamma and screams.

RACHEL: AHHHHH!

Chapter Thirteen
"We All Have a Purpose"

V.O. - As Senar and the gang head south, they exit into a town called Pleasantville New Jersey. They find a house right off the highway and pull into the driveway. Senar and Maggie get out and they see that it's the perfect resting spot. A brick house with very few windows. Senar and Maggie go in, checks out the house and comes back to the car. It's all clear. Everyone goes into the house and they begin boarding up the windows. Everyone huddles up in the middle of the room, leaning on each other for heat. Anyia and Senar step out the front door. They have the first watch.

EXT. PORCH IN PLEASANTVILLE. DAY

ANYIA: Hey good looking. How are your wounds healing?

SENAR: I don't think they are.

ANYIA: Are you in a lot of pain?

SENAR: Only when I breathe.

ANYIA: Well I guess you're going to be in pain the rest of your life.

SENAR: Right! The way things are going that won't be long anyhow.

ANYIA: Don't say that.

SENAR: And your reason is why?

ANYIA: Oh ye who have little faith. Must I show you everything before you believe?

SENAR: Believe in what?

ANYIA: What is to come.

SENAR: Ok, tell me what's coming.

ANYIA: Promise me you will take me seriously.

SENAR: After everything that I have seen tonight and for the last four and half days, why wouldn't I take you seriously?

ANYIA: I keep having a strange vision for some reason.

SENAR: Vision of what?

ANYIA: The vision was clear as day. I saw the clouds open and a great light shined brightly, showing horses and Angels.

SENAR: Word!! I had that same dream last night.

ANYIA: There's something I need to tell you. I haven't told you everything about me.

SENAR: Everything like what?

V.O. – Maggie walks to the door and listens.

ANYIA: It doesn't matter where we go from here, what will be, will be.

SENAR: Meaning what?

ANYIA: Meaning… Do you remember seeing the symbol on the back of my neck?

SENAR: Yeah! What about it?

ANYIA: That's my birth right, not just my birth mark.

SENAR: Here you go, scaring me again. Am I going to need to drink for this one too?

ANYIA: You may need to.

SENAR: Let me guess; you are not from here are you?

ANYIA: You're right, I'm not!

SENAR: Then who are you?

ANYIA: Don't get mad Senar; I see you are getting frustrated.

SENAR: Whatever, get to the point.

V.O. – Maggie briefly interrupts.

MAGGIE: I'll stand watch.

ANYIA: You get some rest.

MAGGIE: No really. I can't sleep right now anyway.

SENAR: Yeah go ahead Anyia; we'll finish this conversation some other time.

ANYIA: (Cutting her eyes at Maggie) Yeah some other time.

INT. LIVING ROOM. DAY

V.O. – Anyia goes back inside. Shelia is awakened by the movement.

SHELIA: I know that look on your face. What's the matter?

ANYIA: I don't think that Senar realizes how important he is.

SHELIA: Come again.

ANYIA: I know who my parents really are.

SHELIA: Look Anyia, I'm your friend, but even I am getting tired of you talking in riddles.

ANYIA: I'm sorry, but it seems like another part of me is taking over.

SHELIA: You know it's strange that you say that because I left home when I was young and my parents told me that I would never amount to nothing. I believed that for so long and even though I'm successful, I still feel like I have served no purpose.

ANYIA: Sometimes our purpose is to ensure the survival of another, that they might do something wonderful.

SHELIA: Wow! I never looked at it that way. Get some sleep while you can Anyia.

ANYIA: You do the same.

SHELIA: Anyia are you scared?

ANYIA: Yes I am.

EXT. PORCH. DUSK

V.O. – Senar and Maggie talked about Anyia outside. A dark cloud begins to cover the whole sky, literally almost blocking out the sun completely. You could hear the thunder roar, but there was no lightning. The rain began to fall. A worried look covered Maggie's face. Senar too looks concerned.

MAGGIE: Ok Senar, Do you notice something different about Anyia?

SENAR: Like what?

MAGGIE: Well like… more and more each day she is beginning to speak in parables. Don't you just find that a little bit odd?

SENAR: You know that is kind of odd and the whole time I've been thinking that she's been talking in riddles.

MAGGIE: I remember Shelia telling me a story about one of her friends from the islands. She said she had two more sisters and a brother, but she only remembers them vaguely.

SENAR: What does that got to do with what we're talking about?

MAGGIE: Maybe a lot, maybe nothing, but I remember Shelia saying that this friend of hers was adopted by Dr. Stevens and that there was something so special about this child that he dedicated his life to protecting her.

SENAR: Ok, once again, what does this got to do with Anyia?

MAGGIE: She said the woman who was her mother was a very special lady in the Channel Islands, but feared for her daughter's life, so she sent her to the states with him.

SENAR: What made him believe?

MAGGIE: He had skin cancer. A week with her and he was cured, not even one remission.

SENAR: So tell me genius girl, how do we know for sure?

MAGGIE: All of the grandmother's descendents had a mark on their necks that was a birth mark in the shape of a butterfly naturally.

SENAR: Ok, Houston we have a problem.

MAGGIE: What Senar?

SENAR: Don't move!

INT. WAR ROOM. NIGHT

Chapter Fourteen
"Faith Is Everything"

V.O. – Meanwhile back at the Pentagon leaving the war room.

PRES. CLAYTON: I hope they will be here soon.

CHOI: I hope so too Sir.

PRES. CLAYTON: They'll be here.

CHOI: Tomorrow is my son's birthday, because of my job I never got to celebrate his birthday with him. I always sent him gifts. We were going fishing tomorrow.

V.P. POOL: Well we all know that's not going to happen unless you're going as bait.

RIVERA: How 'bout I get ya'll some party hats from the dollar store.

CHOI: What?

RIVERA: If you two can get ya'll sentimental heads out of ya'll butts, we can help those people out there dying in the dark.

V.P. POOL: You're out of line Rivera.

RIVERA: Like hell I am. Life as we know it could very well be at its end, so do you really think I care about you, the White House, or anyone else at this moment? The only one I have to answer to after all of this is said and done, is God.

V.O. – The room gets quiet. Carmen grabs her things and leaves.

As if right on cue, good times never last long. As Maggie stands staring in Senar's eyes, the fear that she saw let her know that whatever he was looking at behind her, was something he had never seen before. What stood behind her was a mutated grizzly bear with the head of a lion and wings of an eagle. Before she could turn around, the beast grabbed her with his claws and took off into the air with her. As it ascended towards the tree line, Anyia ran out the house with a grenade launcher.

She fired into the air, piercing the creature's rib cage. Still refusing to let go, Maggie stuck the shotgun to its neck and pulled the trigger, killing the beast instantly. As both fall to the ground, Maggie falls through the trees hitting the ground only after being slowed by the trees. The beast fell dead and impelled itself on the top of the tree that she fell through. Senar comes running through the brush.

EXT. WOODS. NIGHT

SENAR: Maggie! Maggie! Where are you?

V.O. – Anyia comes running through the brush.

ANYIA: Senar! To your left, she fell over to the left.

SENAR: How far?

ANYIA: About a hundred yards.

VO. – Just then Maggie screams out Anyia's name.

MAGGIE: Anyia! I'm over here.

SENAR: Keep talking Maggie.

MAGGIE: Senar! Forget about me. You have to protect Anyia.

V.O. – Senar and Anyia reach Maggie at the same time. Anyia reaches down and puts her hands on Maggie's face.

ANYIA: It's ok Maggie I'm right here, you'll be alright.

MAGGIE: I had a vision when I was falling through the trees.

SENAR: What vision?

MAGGIE: A vision of me being held by an Angel and she told me that everything will be alright. All my life I've been scared of getting close to anybody, because everybody that I love leaves me one way or another; so I stay on the defensive. I stay cold and alone so I don't have to feel for nobody.

SENAR: Ok we can have this conversation somewhere else.

ANYIA: No wait! Senar don't move her.

MAGGIE: I want you to do me one favor Anyia. I know who you are and I'll never tell a soul if you don't want me to, but please don't let me die. I have a purpose now, at least let me die for a purpose. For once in my life I really want to live.

V.O. – (Gasping for air and crying, Maggie fights for her life.)

SENAR: What's wrong Maggie? Anyia what's wrong with her?

ANYIA: Judging from the blood coming from her mouth. She is bleeding internally.

SENAR: We have to do something. We can't just let her die.

ANYIA: Do you really know what love is Senar?

SENAR: What?

ANYIA: What would you give to save her life? Would you give your own?

SENAR: (Pausing for a moment) Yes! Yes I would.

ANYIA: If I show you something Senar I'll expose you to something you have never seen before and then everything that chases me seen and unseen would become your burden too. Now I ask you once again, if it took your last breath to bring her back would you give it?

V.O. - Senar looking up at the sky and then looking down at his daughter's picture turns and looks at Anyia.

SENAR: Promise me one thing.

ANYIA: What's that Senar?

SENAR: Let my baby know that I love her very much and promise me you'll take care of her.

ANYIA: I promise.

SENAR: What you want me to do Anyia?

ANYIA: I need you to lie down next to her and hold her hand.

V.O. - As Senar lies down next to Maggie, Anyia kneels down in between the both of them. She puts her hands on both of their hearts with tears running down her face. She leans over and kisses Senar. As she looks up into the sky, the wind stops blowing and the sky begins to darken. She begins to pray. Our father who art in heaven hallowed be thy name.

Thy kingdom come thy will be done on earth as it is in heaven give us this day our daily bread and forgive us of our trespasses as we forgive those who trespass against us. Lead us not into temptation but deliver us from evil: For thine is the kingdom, the power, and the glory forever Amen.

Just at that moment, the sky lit up with lightning. Anyia's eyes began to roll back in her head. Maggie goes into convulsions. Senar takes his last breath. Anyia's hands light up as if on fire. Maggie and Senar both fall still. Anyia raises her hands up to the sky and says, thank you Jesus, thank you Father God glory be onto you and you are worthy to be praised. The rain begins to fall. Anyia falls limp to the ground. Feeling the water hitting her face Anyia awakens. She touches Maggie's face once again. Wake up Maggie. You're not finished yet. Maggie opens her eyes looks up at Anyia and begins to cry.

MAGGIE: I knew I was right about you.

ANYIA: What do you mean?

MAGGIE: You were the angel in my dream.

V.O. – Maggie looks over and sees Senar lying dead and begins to cry out loud. No No, No.

MAGGIE: No Senar, you can't leave us now. We need you, I need you. Wake up!

MAGGIE: Anyia what happened?

ANYIA: He had a choice between him or you and he chose you.

MAGGIE: But I choose him Anyia, I choose him.

V.O. – (Maggie lay over Senar's chest crying.)

MAGGIE: If this is the price that I must pay to live, I choose not to.

ANYIA: Would you have given your life for him to live?

MAGGIE: In a heartbeat!

ANYIA: Do you believe Jesus is real?

MAGGIE: Yes I do.

ANYIA: Well I leave you to pray and by your faith shall his fate lie.

MAGGIE: What do you mean?

ANYIA: I can only plant the seed. The spirit will water it.

MAGGIE: Help me Anyia. Please help me.

ANYIA: This is your fate, this is your destiny, and this is your purpose.

V.O. – As Anyia walks out of the brush, Maggie begins to pray. Lord, I know I haven't been to you in a long time, but please forgive me. I know those who have left to be with you was your will O Lord, please help Senar, he's just a wretch like me who don't deserve your love, but we are both thankful that you give it. I don't think he's finished yet either. Lord, have mercy on him, Lord and have mercy on me. Please send him back just for a little while longer. In Jesus name I pray. Thank you Father God, thank you for answering my prayers. Maggie turns and looks down at Senar, hoping for the best and there's Senar with his eyes wide open saying......

SENAR: Hey you.

V.O. – Overwhelmed with joy, Maggie leaps on Senar and hugs him.

MAGGIE: I knew we would be alright. Anyia told me in a dream.

SENAR: Okay, can I take a breath first?

MAGGIE: Oops, my bad.

ANYIA: Hey good looking, How are you?

SENAR: I thought I was supposed to be…….

ANYIA: Shhh, don't talk, let's get the hell out of here and I will explain to you later.

MAGGIE: How did I survive?

ANYIA: Senar was willing to give his life for you.

MAGGIE: Did he really do that for me?

ANYIA: Yes he did and the Lord did the rest, and let's not also forget that you were ready to give your life for him too!

SENAR: That's a beautiful thing, so now let's bounce.

V.O. – Chet, Cookie, Toonie, and Kyla all sit in the living room waiting for Senar, Anyia and Maggie's return.

COOKIE: Hey Chet, somebody's coming.

CHET: Who is it?

V.O. – Kyla and Toonie run to the window.

KYLA: Who is that? I can't see.

TOONIE: I know that walk from anywhere. That's my daddy.

COOKIE: I can't see anything.

KYLA: Oh my God! It's Maggie and it looks like she's hurt.

CHET: Open the door. Get the first aid kit. Help them inside.

INT. HOUSE. 1 AM

Day Five

TOONIE: Daddy! Daddy! Are you alright?

SENAR: Yes baby I'm ok.

TOONIE: Good, cause while you were outside playing around, something could have come in here and got me, and then you'd be feeling bad, so you stay where I can see you, so nothing don't get me and you don't have to be feeling bad for me being gone. Ok!

SENAR: Ok baby I promise.

COOKIE: What happened out there Senar?

SENAR: One of the most amazing things I have ever seen in my life.

KYLA: I suppose we need to hold up here until daylight, right. Not that I'm scared or nothing, I just don't see well in the dark. I wear contacts. The doctor said that I got astigmatism.

ANYIA: It's cool Kyla, we're going to stay here till daylight.

SENAR: Word, cause I'm tired.

CHET: Ya'll get some rest. Come here Kyla let me show you how to use a gun.

KYLA: Now that's what's up?

CHET: Me, Kyla, Cookie got watch. Senar keep Toonie with you.

SENAR: Don't give Cookie a gun. I remember her shooting at me twice.

COOKIE: I missed on purpose.

ANYIA: Come on Maggie. Let's lay down. We got another long day tomorrow, I'm sure.

Chapter Fifthteen
"Touched By an Angel"

V.O. – Senar, Anyia, Maggie and Toonie lay in the middle of the circle in the front room on the couches. Another night comes to an end, but it was really only the beginning.

V.O. - Senar still bleeding to death on the roof top looking up at the moon hearing the carnage coming towards him. Senar talking to someone as if he could see them. One would say he's delirious, but some might say otherwise. Some people say that they're afraid to die, but there are so many afraid to live. We would like to choose the way that we die, but we know that that's not possible.

ANYIA: (Sitting up by herself) Hey Toonie pss… tell me you got a pencil.

TOONIE: Girl I never leave home without one. (Laughing out loud) No I'm just playing, here you go.

ANYIA: Thank you.

MAGGIE: What you doing Anyia?

ANYIA: I'm just writing a poem.

MAGGIE: At a time like this?

ANYIA: Yes it relaxes me. I was almost finished, but my pencil broke.

TOONIE: Will you read it to me later?

ANYIA: Sure baby.

MAGGIE: That better be a beautiful poem, writing at a time like this.

ANYIA: It's not exactly a poem. It's something that I would like to say to someone and this is just in case I don't get the chance.

TOONIE: (Laughing) I know who it is. It's my daddy ain't it?

ANYIA: (Laughing) No it ain't and it's time for you to lie down.

TOONIE: Ok.

MAGGIE: Sweet dreams baby.

ANYIAL: Are you alright Maggie?

MAGGIE: I'm better than alright. I feel reborn.

ANYIA: That's good.

MAGGIE: How did you…

ANYIA: Not now Maggie, please.

V.O. – Chet walking over to the girls.

CHET: How ya'll ladies doing?

ANYIA: We're ok.

CHET: We should be able to hold up here until morning.

MAGGIE: If you think so.

ANYIA: I know so.

"And I looked and behold a pale horse and his name that sat on him was death and hell followed with him and power was given onto them over the fourth part of the earth to kill with sword and with hunger and with death and with the beast of the earth."

Revelation 6:8

V.O. – Kyla walks over to Senar to thank him.

KYLA: Hey Senar, how you feeling?

SENAR: I'm straight, just a little sore and wounded, but besides that, everything's fine.

KYLA: Sorry about your friend. I'm sure he was a good man.

SENAR: Yes he was, a very good man.

KYLA: What's going on Senar? What's really happening?

SENAR: I haven't got a clue, ask Anyia or Shelia.

KYLA: You get some rest. I didn't mean to bother you.

SENAR: It's cool; wake me up in an hour.

KYLA: That's what's up.

V.O. – As morning began to rise, everybody meets up outside.

EXT. FRONT YARD. MORNING

ANYIA: Listen up! Everybody get a weapon, everybody stay safe, everybody stay alert.

SENAR: Toonie, you come go with me.

MAGGIE: Me, Anyia and Kyla will ride with you Senar.

SENAR: Alright let's bounce.

V.O. - As the two vehicles speed down the highway, everybody's spirit seemed to be lifted. The sky starts to get dark and a strong breeze begins to blow. Anyia starts to make a transformation and although most people speak of the end, it's for sure that this is the beginning.

EXT. WOODS. DAY

V.O. - Meanwhile the chopper flies high above the dense fog that begins to roll in.

PILOT: Do you see anything?

CO PILOT: No nothing Jim, nothing but fog and dense clouds.

INT. PENTAGON. DAY

V.O. - Meanwhile back at the Pentagon, Carmen Rivera has decided to take matters into her own hands. Carmen Rivera decides to lead the search party heading north up I-95 looking for Anyia and Chet and any other survivors that she could find.

V.O. - Meanwhile death and desolation cover the earth; those who are still alive seemed to be praying for death. Man, nature and God have all decided to come at the same time. No more will we wonder, enjoy your last breath. Carmen Rivera, Sgt. Jones and Sgt. Adams speed up the highway in desperation with one thing in mind, finding Anyia and that canister.

EXT. HIGHWAY. DAY

CARMEN: Sgt. Jones, what does that sign say coming up here on the right?

SGT. JONES: Pleasantville Ma'am.

SGT. ADAMS: Maybe we should take this exit and see if we can find a gas station where we can take some gas.

CARMEN: You know that's stealing soldier.

SGT. JONES: Who's going to tell it anyway?

SGT. ADAMS: You got a point there.

V.O. - Just then something hits the roof of the vehicle, almost turning it over. Carmen struggles to hold control of the vehicle. Something rips through the top of the roof decapitating Sgt. Adams.

Sgt. Jones fires up through the roof repeatedly. The vehicle slides into the gutter. The creature lands on the hood of the car dead. Carmen, visibly shaken, screams out.

CARMEN: What is that?

SGT. JONES: I don't know what it is, but I hope it's dead.

CARMEN: How can you be sure?

SGT. JONES: Well I'm not.

V.O. – He fires ten rounds into the creature.

CARMEN: Let's get the hell out of here.

V.O. – Carmen speeds off shaking the creature off the hood of the car while exiting off the ramp. They get to the gas station, fill up the tank and fill a barrel full of gas. They then speed out the gas station and come to a screeching halt 50 yards away. Using a flare gun to ignite the barrel, Carmen fires at the barrel creating a huge explosion and a massive fire.

CARMEN: Ok what now?

SGT. JONES: We wait.

CARMEN: Wait for who?

SGT. JONES: Wait for a miracle.

CARMEN: I don't think we got that much time.

EXT. HIGHWAY. DUSK

V.O. – Meanwhile Senar and his crew speed down the highway heading south approaching a town called Cherry Hill. The fog is so dense they can barely see.

KYLA: Where the hell are we now?

COOKIE: We ain't in Kansas no more.

CHET: I know we're not too far from D.C.

MAGGIE: I say we pull over.

SHELIA: I think we're better off moving.

SENAR: Good thing we got these two-way radios, because I don't think getting out of the car is an option.

TOONIE: Daddy I'm scared.

ANYIA: I got to pee, so we are going to have to stop.

MAGGIE: Now that she mentioned it, I got to pee too.

SENAR: Alright, we are going to pull over here by this field. Everybody stay alert.

EXT. HIGHWAY. FIELD. SUN DOWN

V.O. – As both vehicles pull over, the fog seems to get thicker and thicker. Senar notices something moving in the fog, but he doesn't want to alarm anybody. Anyia and Maggie squat between the two vehicles to relieve themselves. Cookie and Toonie stand in front of the first vehicle. From out of nowhere a creature runs out of the woods. They begin to fire at it, but it just keeps coming. While everyone is shooting at the creature, another one runs out of the woods and snatches Toonie and takes off running down the trail. Anyia screams out.

ANYIA: Senar they got Toonie, they got Toonie.

V.O. - Toonie screams out daddy help me!

SENAR: Hang on baby, I'm coming for you.

V.O. - As the first creature drops dead, everyone grabs their gun that didn't have one and runs off chasing Senar who's chasing the creature who has Toonie. Senar not able to get a clean shot on the creature, starts firing at the creatures legs, just slowing him down barely. Maggie yells to Anyia…..

MAGGIE: You hear that.

ANYIA: Yeah I hear it, it's a chopper.

CHET: Maggie shoot off a flare.

MAGGIE: Got you.

V.O. - Chet gets on the radio and makes contact with the chopper.

The pilot makes contact with Senar on the radio.

SENAR: Drop me a line, drop me a line.

PILOT: You got it.

V.O. - Senar grabs the line. As the chopper lifts him into the air, the chopper flies him up over the creature, but he still can't get a good shot, Toonie's in the way. A very dense patch of fog envelopes the area. Senar loses sight of the creature and Toonie. He screams out her name frantically, but to no avail. The creature runs through the bush with Toonie in tow, but then it suddenly stopped in its tracks. Sheer fear lights up the creature's face. A bright light and an Angel appear before him as Toonie falls to the ground. The creature stands in sheer terror and tries to run, but is blown apart by the Angel. Just then Senar appears out the fog, while still hanging on to the line. He sees Toonie lying on the ground. After witnessing what the Angel did to the creature, he lets go of the line falling to the ground unable to move. He just lies there as tears roll down his face. Deep down he had always had faith and now knowing what he knows, the sheer joy is overwhelming.

"And if any man will hurt them fire proceedth out of their mouth and devoured their enemies and if any man will hurt them he must in this manner be killed."

Rev. 11:5

"And when they shall have finished their testimony, the beast that ascendeth out of the bottomless pit shall make war against them, and shall overcome them, and kill them."

Rev. 11:7

V.O. - Senar, feeling truly humbled, lays his head on the ground and begins to say thank you Jesus thank you Lord. The angel lays Toonie at Senar's head and says to him.

ANGEL: "Cry no more for he has come to wipe away your tears."

V.O. - Anyia comes through the brush and falls to the ground as if dead.

ANGEL: "Protect her, she is who she is, let your faith be your guide."

V.O. - A loud sonic boom explodes through the air as the Angel departs. The helicopter and the rest of the crew arrive at the scene at the same time to find Anyia, Senar and Toonie lying as if dead. Cookie races to Toonie....

COOKIE: Toonie baby, wake up baby.

MAGGIE: Senar, Anyia please wake up please!

TOONIE: Hey mama!

COOKIE: Hey baby.

TOONIE: Is daddy alright?

MAGGIE: He's alright and Anyia is fine too!

SENAR: Did ya'll see that?

SHELIA: See what Senar?

SENAR: Never mind.

ANYIA: I saw it Senar, and it was beautiful.

TOONIE: I saw it too!

KYLA: I didn't see anything and unless we all want to be seeing black I suggest that we get out of here.

CHET: Ok let's move out.

V.O. - As they walk back through the brush to the vehicles, Kyla sees something in the bushes. As the moon comes up, you could see movement all throughout the brush. They were in the midst of a breeding ground; Kyla walks back side by side with Maggie.

MAGGIE: Kyla you see that?

KYLA: See what?

MAGGIE: I know I'm not tripping.

KYLA: Wait a minute I do see it. What the hell is that?

MAGGIE: Senar I think we got company.

SENAR: Lock and load.

CHET: Everyone watch your back.

SHELIA: Oh my God they're everywhere.

COOKIE: Toonie stay by my side.

ANYIA: Quick! Everybody form a circle back to back.

SENAR: Everybody keep firing, Kyla keep everybody with a clip.

CHET: Do not break formation.

V.O. - As the creatures advance slowly around them, everything seems to slow down. It will take a miracle for them to live through this. Senar gets a call on the radio. It's the chopper.

PILOT: Chet, stay back I am going to light a fire around you.

CHET: Roger that.

V.O. - As the fire engulfs them, they continue to shoot through the fire and at anything that's moving. They hear the wonderful sound of the chopper's guns mowing down the creatures ten by ten.

ANYIA: Something just flew over us Senar.

SENAR: Shelia, watch our top.

SHELIA: Top, what do you mean top?

MAGGIE: Look up, Look up!

TOONIE: Mommy I'm scared.

ANYIA: Stay down Shelia, Stay down.

SHELIA: They're everywhere. There's too many of them.

ANYIA: Keep your eyes up Shelia!

V.O. - Panicking and bordering on hysteria, Shelia stands up and backs away from the circle shooting frantically in the air. Senar moves to get her, but he is too late. Two creatures, one from the air and one from the ground grab her at the same time. Shelia's body splits in two pieces. Each creature leaves with a half. Anyia screams, shooting at each creature in anger and crying out Shelia's name.

ANYIA: Shelia, Noooo!

MAGGIE: Man, we're never going to make it out of here alive.

KYLA: I don't want to die, I don't want to die.

SENAR: Everybody get a grip! Just do what I tell you and we will make it out of here.

CHET: (On the radio with the chopper) Drop a line, drop a line.

PILOT: Roger that.

V.O. – The chopper drops a line and they climb up in the chopper one by one. After everyone makes it in safely, they head south following the highway on the way to the Capital. Anyia visibly upset still crying out Shelia's name. Senar holds her and says nothing. Toonie leaves Cookie's embrace to go comfort Anyia and she says.

TOONIE: It will be alright Anyia.

KYLA: How do you know?

TOONIE: An angel told me and the other angel saved me from the monster.

ANYIA: I know it will be alright Toonie; it's just that I will miss her so much.

TOONIE: Is she with God now?

ANYIA: Yes she is baby.

TOONIE: Then we will see her again?

ANYIA: Yes we will.

SENAR: I never thought that I would ever see some of the things that I have seen the last several days. Un-freaking believable, the Lord sent me an Angel and now I see what my mama use to tell me about faith. Faith is everything.

ANYIA: Senar, more than just your faith is at work here, something big is going on.

SENAR: What's up with that birth mark, its glowing?

"After this I beheld and lo a great multitude, which no man could number, of all nations, and kindreds, and people, and tongues, stood before the throne, and before the Lamb, clothed with white robes, and palms in their hands. And cried with a loud voice, saying, Salvation to our God which sitteth upon the throne, and unto the Lamb."

Revelation 7:9, 10

V.O. – Senar and his battle worn crew fly over the highway heading south.

Chapter Sixteen
"All Together Now"

EXT. SIDE OF HIGHWAY. NIGHT

V.O. – Meanwhile, Carmen Rivera and Sgt. Jones sit on top of the hood of the vehicle having a conversation about life.

SGT. JONES: I bet you have been wondering why I just chose to sit here huh?

CARMEN: Yes I have.

SGT. JONES: I remember when I was young and looking for somebody and I never found them as long as I walked around looking for them, but the moment I got still, they walked up and tapped me on the shoulder.

CARMEN: So you really believe standing still that we'll find them?

SGT. JONES: Yeah I really believe it.

CARMEN: Then I pray that you know what you're talking about.

SGT. JONES: Leave it to me to find out that there are politicians who believe in God. You come off to me like someone who only believes in her abilities.

CARMEN: Yes I'm not perfect. I have done and seen a lot of things that I can't change.

SGT. JONES: Sounds like guilt to me.

CARMEN: The only thing that I am admitting to is that I didn't always do everything the right way, but I am trying to now.

SGT. JONES: What's your story? Why you leave the Pentagon to be out here?

CARMEN: I just couldn't go along with their crap anymore.

SGT. JONES: So you are saying that all of this is one big lie?

CARMEN: You know how it is with the government. You never really know the truth.

SGT. JONES: So Ma'am, tell me how is your faith?

CARMEN: Not as strong as it used to be.

SGT. JONES: You hear that?

CARMEN: Hear what?

SGT. JONES: Sounds like a chopper off in the distance.

CARMEN: Are you serious, because I don't hear anything?

V.O. - Breaking through the clouds of fog is the spotlight from the chopper being drawn to the fire like flies. The Pilot sees the fire and both Carmen Rivera and Sgt. Jones. He lands the chopper. Senar jumps out of the chopper to help the two survivors on the ground. Anyia is right behind him with the canister in hand.

SENAR: Are you guys alright?

SGT. JONES: A little beat up and a little shook up, but besides that we're fine.

V.O. – Jones reaches out to shake Senar's hand.

SGT.JONES: I'm Sgt. Jones and this is Secretary of State Carmen Rivera.

V.O. – Carmen reaches out her hand.

CARMEN: You are a sight for sore eyes.

SENAR: It's my pleasure Ma'am. This is Anyia and my name is Senar.

CARMEN: The Anyia?

ANYIA: Excuse me.

CARMEN: Your name has come up in quite a few conversations young lady. It is my pleasure to finally meet you.

SENAR: Wow!

JONES: What I tell you about faith.

ANYIA: Why would my name come up in y'all conversations?

CARMEN: You have the canister, don't you?

SENAR: Yeah we got it.

JONES: Can we talk about this in the chopper? We do need a ride.

CARMEN: I have so many questions for you Anyia.

ANYIA: Here take the canister.

CARMEN: Do I really want it.

ANYIA: My spirit tells me it's time for you to have it because my burden is much bigger than this canister can hold.

CARMEN: I really do believe your burden is a lot bigger than this canister, but we're half way there now.

ANYIA: Yes we are, ok let's get out of here before more trouble finds us.

CARMEN: I'm right behind you.

SENAR: I hope you haven't been waiting long.

CARMEN: It seems like forever.

SENAR: We would have been here sooner, but we had guests along the way.

CHET: Let's not make this a date; let's get in the air and to the Pentagon.

ANYIA: Good idea.

Day Six

INT. PENTAGON. SUB LEVEL. MIDNIGHT

V.O. - As they land at the Pentagon, a special team waits for the toxins. They grab it from Carmen as soon as she touches down. They rush it into the lab. Everyone is excited in anticipation of the hope that it provides. The day drags on as though time was standing still. While waiting, everyone got a chance to freshen up and to meet at the diner to have something to eat. All of the food is vacuum packed, but least it's something. After eating a meal, Carmen takes them 30 stories below to a room not many people know about. She sits them all down to totally get a grasp on what has been happening out in the field. After Chet, Senar and Anyia finish filling her in on all the exploits that has just been taken place, she sits there speechless. Anyia stands up and begins to start to talk as her tattoo begins to glow even brighter, so bright that everyone notices it.

ANYIA: While we've been ending one war, another one is starting.

SENAR: Ok, this can't be good.

ANYIA: Don't be afraid, for they will come for us, because the light is with us. Our sacrifice will not be in vain.

SENAR: Hey Chet, is it just me or is her tattoo glowing?

CHET: Oh boy, I was hoping I was just tired, but thanks for confirming that some more crap is about to go down.

V.O. - VP Pool, Pres. Clayton, and Sec. Of Defense Choi enters the room.

CHOI: Where's my son?

CHET: I am sorry sir, he didn't make it.

CHOI: My boy he's…

CHET: Yes Sir, I am afraid so.

V.O. – Carmen walks over to Choi and hugs him and whispers something in his ear.

CARMEN: We'll see him soon.

V.O. – Lu Choi breaks out crying uncontrollably. He lies on the floor and bawls like a baby. Anyia kneels down and puts her hand on his face and says, "He will take your hurt away" and then immediately he stopped crying and looked at her in disbelief.

"For the Lamb which is in the midst of the throne shall feed them, and shall lead them unto living fountains of waters and God shall wipe away all tears from their eyes."

Revelation 7:17

V.O. – Senar, Carmen, and Maggie step off to the side to discuss what they have just witnessed.

MAGGIE: Tell me I'm not the only one who just saw that.

CARMEN: Please forgive me, but I know somebody has something to sip on.

SENAR: What?

MAGGIE: Well, it would be nice to have something to relax our nerves.

SENAR: Well I got a little something for you.

V.O. – (While laughing hysterically)

CARMEN: No, I'm serious. I need a drink.

SENAR: Ok, I'll drink while ya'll figure out what the heck is going on with Anyia.

MAGGIE: So, do you really think she is the one that will save us all?

CARMEN: As much as I hate to say it, I think she is.

SENAR: What's up with that light on her neck?

V.P. POOL: Maybe we should throw some holy water on her.

SENAR: Can you give us a minute here? Thank you. We appreciate it.

V.P. POOL: Well what about her?

CARMEN: I'll take care of her. You just go have a seat.

MAGGIE: So is she… do you really think she is the one?

CARMEN: You've seen what she can do.

MAGGIE: If she saves us, what then?

SENAR: Maybe she's not supposed to save us; maybe she is supposed to show us how to save ourselves.

CARMEN: How do you mean save us?

V.O. – Senar, staring at the bottle of Jack Daniels, but not having the urge to drink anymore. Not even he knows why.

SENAR: Think about it.

MAGGIE: Well maybe she'll just lead the way.

CARMEN: Lead the way where? Exactly where are we going?

SENAR: Heaven!

V.O. - Everybody stands there stunned.

V.O. - The lab techs come back from the lab with the results. They were able to isolate the spores. Now they just need a way to disperse them.

Chapter Seventeen
"Trojan Horse"

Meanwhile, Pentagon cameras pick up a little boy and a dog on the Pentagon's lawn running through the front gate. He seems to be screaming something as he gets closer to the Pentagon. A camera further down the road picks up what is chasing him. Dozens of the creatures were not far behind him. Somebody informs Chet over the radio of the situation. Chet, Senar and Sgt. Jones rush towards the door to try and save the boy. Just as the boy almost reaches the door, one of the creatures leaps out at him. At the same time the dog leaps at the creature, but it split the dog in half. Senar and Chet open up the door and opens fire on the creature while Sgt. Jones snatches the boy through the door. Hundreds of creatures are behind him.

INT. LOBBY. PENTAGON. PRE DAWN

SENAR: Chet fall back, fall back.

JONES: I got the boy.

CHET: What the heck are you doing out there?

BOY: I'm here for a purpose.

CHET: What's that?

V.O. – Senar turning around; screamed.

SENAR: Nooooo!

V.O. – Just then the boy changes into his real form. Using his tentacles to rip Jones from the inside out, it immediately turns on Chet. As he begins to open fire, one of the tentacles puts a deep gash in his right leg. Senar begins shooting the creature, running at it with everything he's got. Another creature breaks through the door and more follow after him. Chet hangs on Senar's shoulder while still loading his clip with one hand. Senar and Chet back towards the elevator to the sub basement, but Senar can't move but so fast while having Chet on his arm. He gives Chet one of his guns and puts it in his other hand while firing in front of him, running full speed towards the elevator dragging Chet behind. Chet's leaving a trail of blood behind him while firing at everything leaping at him.

Just as he's almost to the elevator, one of the big creatures leaps between him and the elevator. Just as he raises his tentacles to rip Senar in half, his whole head is blown off from behind. The creature falls on top of Senar and Chet. Looking up at the elevator, Senar sees Anyia standing in the doorway with the door wide open with a rocket launcher in her hand still smoking.

ANYIA: Going down?

SENAR: Yes please!

INT. ELEVATOR. DAWN

V.O. - Senar kicks the body off of him and Chet and drags Chet into

the elevator and they begin to head down.

SENAR: How many times are you going to save my life?

ANYIA: As many times as I have to.

SENAR: Why me?

ANYIA: Why not you?

SENAR: Do you know the kind of life that I led?

ANYIA: The first shall be last and the last shall be first.

CHET: Can I get some help here. A tourniquet would be nice.

V.O. - Anyia ties a tourniquet around Chet's leg and gives him a shot from her bag. The elevator doors open and two technicians grab hold of Chet and put him on the stretcher. They have been watching the whole thing on a monitor.

INT. SUB LEVEL. TRIAGE. DAWN

V.O. - Toonie runs and grabs her father and hugs him real tight. They go sit down and not a word is said. Maggie says a prayer for Sgt. Jones and for Chet.

SENAR V.O. – (Present Day) Today might be my last day on earth but now at least I can go in peace. I see there is a lot more to life than I originally had thought. I see that God has mercy on us all and I am blessed to take each breath. I never realized how hope is everything till now. Anyia showed me how to the Lord we all are important and he loves all of us the same.

KYLA: Hey ya'll. I don't want to rain on your parade, but I think we ought to be leaving.

MAGGIE: Let's use the tunnel.

CARMEN: Grab everything that you can carry.

ANYIA: We have time to pray don't we?

SENAR: That sounds good to me.

V.P. POOL: Somebody needs to get this to Capt Lucas right away.

V.O. – Just then several secret service men walk through the adjacent doors. Pres. Clayton was right behind them.

PRES. CLAYTON: Yes. We should be going, but first where is she?

CHOI: Where is who Sir?

PRES.CLAYTON: My daughter.

CARMEN: What the heck is he talking about?

CLAYTON: Where is she?

CHOI: That's not your daughter Sir. She's a clone.

CARMEN: Oh my God!

CLAYTON: I am not going to ask you again.

POOL: She's in B-wing Sir.

V.O. – Pres. Clayton and his men proceed back down the hall to B-wing. As he turns the corner, he sees the girl who was cloned from his daughter. She runs towards him, but then there's a big boom and an earth shaking roar. As the building crumbles around them, they decide that it's time to go.

CHOI: Leave me here I don't want to go on.

TOONIE: You have to go on.

COOKIE: Baby, he's just tired that's all.

CHET: I'm dying over here. Can I have some drugs please?

CARMEN: We're going to Capt. Lucas' Lab so we can find a way to disperse the toxin.

SENAR: You heard the lady. Let's go!

ANYIA: We have to get out of here Senar!

SENAR: Why, what's your hurry?

ANYIA: I feel something coming; you're going to have to trust me.

KYLA: Did you feel that? It felt like something big hit the earth.

V.P. POOL: I did feel something.

V.O. - Boom! A loud and horrific quake follows the explosion.

SENAR V.O. - I remember it so clearly. We had just gone through the doors to the Lab when another big boom hit, and then the Pentagon behind us was gone. The heat was intense and we ran down the corridor through the doors that waited opened for us by two armed guards.

We barely made it in before the searing heat burned us to death. I looked back to see if everybody made it and to my sadness, everyone didn't. Cookie had run back to help V.P. Pool and she had been torched by the heat wave that followed the meteor that hit first. VP Pool tried to carry her out, but he too was overwhelmed by the fire.

V.O. – Meanwhile in Heaven

"And the Great dragon was cast out that old serpent called the Devil and Satan which decevith the whole world, he was cast out into the earth and his angels were cast out with him. And I heard a loud voice saying in Heaven, now is come salvation and strength and the kingdom of our God and the power of his CHRIST for the accuser of our brethen is cast down, which accused them before our God day and night."

Rev. 12: 9, 10

SENAR V.O. – Cookie is dead and now once again we begin to wander through all the carnage and chaos that surrounds us. We finally make it to Capt. Lucas' lab.

INT. LUCAS LAB. SUNRISE

V.O. – Senar and the gang talk to Capt. Lucas.

ANYIA: You must be Capt Lucas.

CAPT. LUCAS: Yes I am and you must be Anyia.

MAGGIE: Cookie and Pool, where are they?

CHET: They didn't make it?

TOONIE: No, my mommy!

SENAR: Come here Toonie.

V.O. – Senar picks Toonie up and holds her tight.

SENAR: I love you baby, you know that, right? She's with the Angels now.

TOONIE: You mean that Angel that saved me?

ANYIA: Yeah! That's the one.

MAGGIE: The lab said they have loaded the toxin on the missile and they are ready to launch.

KYLA: Let's get a game plan.

CARMEN: O.K. did you hear that?

KYLA: That's what I've been trying to tell you.

CHOI: I think they are getting through!

CHET: Let's get out of here.

V.O. – Just then Pres. Clayton staggers through the doors holding the dead body of his daughter.

PRES. CLAYTON: I'm not going anywhere.

SENAR: And to think I almost voted for you.

ANYIA: Leave him.

KYLA: Let's go.

Chapter Eighteen
"Greater Is He That Is In Me"

EXT. HUMMER. SUNRISE

Senar V. O. – We all left through the tunnel and hopped in the hummer heading west. We can see the missile launch and it lights up the sky. Ground zero should be somewhere in Alaska, so the toxin can spread on the northern jet stream. I thought that everything was over when we saw something standing in the road. I couldn't believe what I was seeing. I never thought that I would see a snake that big in real life or on T. V. I hit the brakes and Anyia's neck began to glow like brass. We jumped out shooting with little effect.

EXT. HIGHWAY. MORNING

Senar V.O. – I knew this was going to be one of those moments you would never forget. The snake rose up high in the air and said.

SNAKE: I have been looking for you. Sssssss!

ANYIA: In the name of Jesus, I command you to leave us and go hence away from here."

SNAKE: You dare defy me; I will torment you a thousand ways.

ANYIA: You know not where my sister is at or you would not be here.

SNAKE: I see you have favor sssssssssssss, but you have no power over me.

ANYIA: But my father does.

V.O. – Senar and the rest of the crew were scared to death, but Anyia wasn't.

ANYIA: I know you have sent your flood after her and the earth has swallowed it up, then you tried to kill her and the man child that she carries, but her wings carried her away to the wilderness where you now hunt her seed. I indeed know who you are and I too have been waiting for you!

SNAKE: We will sssssssssee!

V.O. – The snake opened up its bowels to let out demons from within. Anyia raised her arms up and said something in some ancient tongue and all of the demons froze and then blew up. Anyia eyes began to glow and the snake grew angrier.

SNAKE: I will come for you and I will torment you forever.

ANYIA: Go hence away from us!

V.O. – The snake leaves and Anyia falls to the ground. She wakes up with no memory of what just happened. All who have seen this will never forget it. As they pick Anyia off of the ground, the toxins began to have an effect on the aliens that were attacking us before. They were on the ground convulsing. The one thing that we forgot was that the manmade mutations might be harder to kill.

SENAR: Everybody to the truck.

INT. TRUCK. HIGHWAY. MORNING

CARMEN: Where's the President?

SENAR: He chose to stay where he thought it was safe.

CARMEN: Oh! Yeah! That's right, now I remember. He sucked as a President, but he wasn't as bad as Bush.

KYLA: Come on, I'll help Anyia.

CHOI: Maybe we should get further away from here and find some safety somewhere.

CHET: That's a good idea.

MAGGIE: I just need to get some sleep.

TOONIE: I just want my mommy.

ANYIA: Come to me my child.

Senar V.O. – Anyia holds Toonie real tight and she stops crying and hums the most beautiful thing I have ever heard. Flying down the road in a hurry to nowhere, we just wanted to be anywhere that we could rest. The sun was about to set again and I felt like I was quickly heading towards day seven and if it's like the last six days, God help us all.

"And I stood upon the sand of the sea, and saw a beast rise up out of the sea, having seven heads and ten horns, and upon his horns ten crowns and upon his heads the name of blasphemy."

Rev. 13: 1

Chapter Nineteen
"Revenge Is Not Mine"

SENAR V.O. - As they sped west, everyone couldn't help but to notice that many people are coming out of hiding and trying to help kill off the weakening aliens due to the missile launch exploding in Alaska. It has already killed off most of the creatures. The only ones that should survive were the hybrids and that's a horse of a different color. Flying down the highway heading west, we needed to find something that we could eat. I was starting to feel the infection from my wounds.

Senar V.O. - I didn't know why Anyia wanted to go west, but I figured she knew where she was going. My spirit was telling me to trust her, especially after what I'd already seen. As we headed down the highway, the skies began to turn gray. We could see people scattered here and there. I remember Anyia telling me that things will get worse before they get better, boy was she right!

"And the beast which I saw was like unto a leopard, and his feet were as the feet of a bear, and his mouth as the mouth of a lion: and the dragon gave him his power, and his seat, and great authority."

Rev. 13: 2

MAGGIE: What's going on Anyia?

ANYIA: The war in heaven has come to earth!

SENAR: So what does that all mean?

ANYIA: That means now there will be other creatures that will be after us.

KYLA: Well I gotta pee real bad!

TOONIE: I'm hungry, and I gotta pee too!

CARMEN: Yeah I need to wash this wound for Chet.

CHOI: I think we all could use a break to mourn to ourselves!

CHET: I need more drugs.

KYLA: I gotta 211 in my purse, you can have that!

SENAR: I think that's a fire up ahead. Lock and load people! Maggie, Kyla stay with Toonie and Chet, no matter what happens.

ANYIA: I'm going with you.

CHOI: I'm going too.

MAGGIE: What? Sir we need you to stay here.

CHOI: They killed my freaking son! Now give me a gun, a big one.

CARMEN: Here you go Choi, take mine.

CHOI: I don't want to take your only gun.

CARMEN: I got three more, see. (Opening up her vest).

EXT. SUV. CONVIENCE STORE. NOON

ANYIA: Alright come on, hop out, and let's see what we can find.

KYLA: Yeah I'm gonna find me some Doritos. I never thought I would miss those things!

SENAR: Yeah I like the ranch.

CARMEN: Me, Senar, Anyia, and Choi we'll search the mini mart to see what we can find.

SENAR: Where are we anyway?

CHET: Somewhere by Arkansas.

ANYIA: Ok, lock the doors. Let's roll. Kyla you stay here.

SENAR: We need you to help with Chet and Toonie. Guard them with your life.

KYLA: Word, so this is like an assignment or something?

ANYIA: Yes, Kyla please do this for me!

KYLA: Alright!

V.O. – Carmen, Choi, Anyia and Senar run to the front door of the mini-mart. Not knowing what to expect, they huddle up in front. Anyia let Senar know that there was a creature on the roof. Senar stepped back, and then fired into the air. Choi, eager for some revenge runs through the double doors and opens fire on the creatures inside. Senar screams out for him to wait, but he presses forward doing great damage along the way.

Senar V.O. – I remember that moment when I saw Choi try to take all of his anger out on everything, but then I realized that he was fulfilling his purpose. He didn't care whether he lived or died. He said one thing to me that chilled me to the bone. He said, "If you had to live your life only to give it would you do it?" and I paused for a moment before I answered him because I never thought that I would have to think about it in that way. Choi gave me the question and I had the answer. Yes I would! As I ran through the store shooting everything that moved, I felt no fear because I felt where he was coming from. As Choi turned down the next isle, I saw something grab him and pull him through the ceiling. He was still shooting when he went through the hole. Carmen couldn't leave without her friend. She began to fire up through the hole, only to never see him or the creature again. Anyia ran and grabbed Carmen and pulled her towards the front doors. Senar set off two hand grenades behind him as they all run towards the door. Kicking the front door open, Anyia yells to Maggie to start the truck, "They're right behind us." They jump in the truck and speed off down the highway, running over everything in their path.

INT. HIGHWAY. SUV. DAY

SENAR: How far to the coast Anyia?

ANYIA: Not far!

CARMEN: We need to go back for Choi!

ANYIA: He's gone Carmen for now.

CARMEN: (Crying and screaming) We have to go back, we have to go back!

SENAR: He wanted to go out like a soldier.

MAGGIE: I guess ya'll ain't getting nothing to eat then?

TOONIE: Yeah where's the food dad?

ANYIA: We are the food, the food that feeds the earth!

KYLA: Here we go again, riddle me this? How do we survive?

SENAR: We won't!

Chapter Twenty
"It's A Dog's World"

EXT. NEVEDA DESERT. SUN DOWN

V.O. - Meanwhile Chad and Dana listen for any signs of life as they sit wondering if anyone else is alive. They had just moved out west not long ago. They had to hide in a cave to escape the cross breeds that have been roaming the area. Chad thought it might be best if they tried to go down the mountain to find food and water, it's been three days since they had food and two days without water.

DANA: What are we going to do once we get down hill?

CHAD: We're going to find some food, anything, I just don't want to sit here and starve to death.

DANA: It was your bright idea in the first place to move out here.

CHAD: It really doesn't matter where we live right now, do it?

DANA: Don't get smart with me, I didn't say let's head for the freaking hills did I?

CHAD: What was that?

DANA: What was what?

CHAD: That growling sound.

DANA: Oh! My God! Run Chad! Don't look back!

CHAD: I'm right behind you.

V.O. - Chad and Dana run frantically down the mountain until they get to the road at the bottom. They turn to see what was chasing them and see nothing. Dana walks down the yellow line talking to herself. Chad is right behind her.

CHAD: Dana slow down!

DANA: Oh! NO! Not never! You better walk faster!

V.O. – Dana sees a light coming at them. She turns to tell Chad to come on, but he is not there.

EXT. HIGHWAY. SUV. NIGHT

V.O. – Meanwhile Senar and the gang fly down the highway heading west through the desert. As they turn the corner, they see a girl in the middle of the road. Maggie slams on the brakes to avoid hitting the girl. She runs to the truck screaming that her boyfriend was eaten by something and that they were after her. Senar jumps out running towards her. He raises his gun as if he was about to shoot her, but at the last second he reaches out to her and grabbed her by the arm, swung her around behind him and fired at this creature that was part bear and tiger. Senar kept on shooting, but the creature was still coming. Out of nowhere, Kyla jumps up on top of the truck and fires a grenade launcher directly at the creature's legs blowing them off. The creature came to rest right at Senar's feet and looked up at Senar. Senar decides to have a few parting words for the creature.

EXT. MIDDLE OF ROAD. NIGHT

SENAR: Take me to your leader. (Laughing while looking at the creature) I always wanted to say that.

ANYIA: Everybody get in! Let's get out of here, like now!

SENAR: Aight! Before we go, I'd like to give a shout out to all my creatures that are not here.

V.O. – Senar then blows the creature's head off.

SENAR: Starting with this one here.

ANYIA: We don't have time to play Senar, we need to be going.

SENAR: Let's go, I'm through.

ANYIA: What's your name?

DANA: Dana. (Crying)

ANYIA: Come on Dana get in the truck.

CARMEN: I got her.

MAGGIE: Here they come!

V.O. – They all pile in and speed away heading west; Dana tells about how they were living in the cave and how they had just come down to find food and water. Back in the cave, a large creature drags a barely alive Chad deep into the back of the cave. There sat a woman perched on a rock dressed in all black and wearing the seal of the Vatican. The creature drops Chad in front of her. The woman then drops down and leans over Chad. She then covers his mouth with hers and begins to start absorbing his soul. Then she begins to devour the body.

EXT. BEACH. NIGHT

V.O. – Meanwhile, it's raining on the coast of California. The seas are rough and the wind is blowing. Today would be like no day ever seen before. Two stray dogs search for food along the beach. They walk like they have no care in the world, not knowing that this would be the last time that they will be able to look for food or that their freedom would be taken away from them. One dog sniffs something that looks slimy, creepy, but all so tasty. Having not eaten for days, the one dog begins to eat.

The other dog senses something wrong and begins to turn the other way. The clouds begin to move, the water begins to boil. A giant wave rolls towards the beach and in the midst of the wave comes Satan himself in all his beastly form. Just as the dog was walking away, Satan himself comes out the water and snatches the dog in its mouth, while he frantically tries to fight his way out the devil's mouth. No match for the devil, he is eaten instantly. The other dog barks and whines while he watches his friend being taken away. While backing away, he bumps into something. As he turns around he saw another creature with horns on his head and drool coming from his mouth, waiting to eat the dog, but instead decided that he may come in handy and takes on the life form of the dog.

V.O. – Meanwhile Senar and his crew drive down the California roads watching the amazing view of the beach, knowing real soon that this will all disappear. Suddenly Senar slams on brakes when he almost runs over a dog that walks in the middle of the road.

EXT. HIGHWAY. NIGHT

SENAR: Oh my God! Everybody hold on. (While swerving the car trying to avoid the dog)

MAGGIE: He came out of nowhere.

ANYIA: Wait don't stop. (Staring the dog in his eyes)

KYLA: What's wrong Anyia? He looks so cute. We can't leave him out here.

DANA: I'm going to go get him.

ANYIA: Nooo! Dana wait.

V.O. – Just then the dog turns into its creature form. Senar yells out, "What the hell?" Everyone reached for their guns! "Shoot it, shoot it," Anyia screamed. Shots rang out and the creature moved fast, it looked like nothing they had ever seen before. Meanwhile guns blazing, Anyia kicks out the windshield. Senar yells out to Toonie to get down and cover her head as they continue to fire at the creature. Not doing any damage, you could see the fear in their eyes. The more they shoot the more it keeps coming.

KYLA: Oh my God!

MAGGIE: We need more ammo.

CHET: Put it in reverse! Put it in reverse!

V.O. - As the vehicle flies backwards, they continued shooting forward as the creature continued to keep coming. Senar says to Anyia, nothing seems to be putting a dent in this thing. Anyia says....

ANYIA: In the mighty name of Jesus go hence where you came from.

SENAR: How do we kill it?

ANYIA: It's not up to us. It's not a physical battle. It's a spiritual battle. Only our faith can save us now.

MAGGIE: So this is it.

KYLA: Stop the truck. I'm gonna buy you some time.

CARMEN: What are you talking about Kyla?

EXT. MIDDLE OF ROAD. NIGHT

V.O. - Anyia steps out of the truck, lifts her hands to the heavens

and claps her hands together. A loud roar covers the whole area. The wind is blowing hard and trees are bending and the sky opens up and what happens next, no one was prepared for. Toonie lifts her head up with tears on her face. Chet holds on to her tight. Kyla jumps out of the vehicle with plastic explosives in her hand and a remote switch.

KYLA: Get out of here Anyia! (With no response from Anyia.)

CARMEN: Get over here Kyla, no don't do it.

KYLA: (Turning around yelling) I finally know what my purpose is.

V.O. - Senar runs and grabs Anyia, but is blown backwards. Maggie yells for everyone to get back in the vehicle. Toonie calls out, "Daddy" as he lies still. Carmen rushes out calling Senar's name. Senar slowly moves. Carmen pulls him back into the truck. Meanwhile Kyla turns and faces Satan himself and begins to pray. The fear on her face is unimaginable and then a peaceful calm overcame her. She suddenly realized she was right where she needed to be. The beast snatched her up and looks her straight in her eyes.

SATAN: Do you know what I am going to do to you? I will devour your soul.

KYLA: I hope you like dark meat and I hope you like it hot.

V.O. - Satan laughs as she quotes out a scripture.

KYLA: As I walk through the valley of the shadow of death, I will fear no evil as she hits the switch.

V.O. - The bomb goes off not killing him, but weakening his physical form. He then summons his demons. They form themselves straight from the earth. Anyia stood there, while the butterfly on her neck created a shield around her. Carmen says....

CARMEN: Oh my God. She gave her life for us.

ANYIA: (Finally breaking her silence) We all have a purpose.

TOONIE: Did my mommy have a purpose too?

MAGGIE: Yes baby, we all have a purpose.

CHET: And to think at one time I didn't believe in God. Lord forgive me.

TOONIE: Daddy you alright?

SENAR: What did I miss?

V.O. - The butterfly on Anyia's neck continued to glow as bright as a star. The wind stopped blowing, the trees got still. Chet and Senar ferociously fought off demons, keeping them from entering the truck, while Maggie fought to protect Toonie from the outside. Everything seemed to move in slow motion. Time seemed to stand still. Maggie watched in horror while Chet was snatched from the truck. Toonie grabbed Chet's hand; Chet grabbed the back of the vehicle to keep from being torn out momentarily. He looks at Toonie with a smile and says it's alright baby, you can let go. Toonie looks up with tears running down her face as he is ripped from her grip. Maggie runs and grabs Toonie just before one of the demons grabs her.

Senar runs towards Maggie and Toonie. There's a demon right behind him. Maggie turns back and realizes escape isn't possible. She then grabs Toonie to her chest gripping her coat tightly. She spins and does a 360 and slings Toonie into the air. One of the demons tries to grab Toonie out of the air. Dana jumps in front of the demon and shoots it with her grenade launcher. Senar catches Toonie while Carmen shoots at the creature about to attack Maggie. Dana takes a vicious blow from one of the demons. Carmen shoots and kills it before it is able to do any more damage. Maggie looks at Carmen and winks, then turns, faces the demons, holds her arms out and looks up to the sky then takes one deep last breath.

Just as she is devoured by the demons, Carmen, Senar, Toonie all scream out. Maggie! Anyia speaks out loud......

ANYIA: "And thus I saw the horses in the vision, and them that sat on them, having breastplates of fire, and of jacinth, and brimstone: and the heads of the horses were as the heads of lions; and out of their mouths issued fire and smoke and brimstone. By these three the third part of men killed."

Revelation 9:17

INT. SUV. NIGHT

V.O. - Senar whipped the SUV around and grabbed Anyia. Everyone jumped in. They take off flying down the road while Anyia starts speaking in a different tongue.

Chapter Twenty One
"The Time Is At Hand"

V.O. – Meanwhile all that were not dead and had not repented was killed by the plagues and the beast that was let loose upon the earth to do God's will as in Revelations. Senar, Anyia, Carmen, Dana and Toonie take a moment to reflect on the events that had just taken place. Anyia begins to pray out loud, looking up at the sky. Toonie is almost in shock, so she holds on to her daddy's arm tight. Senar can't help but to think about the lives that were just lost and how they all gave their life unselfishly and without pause.

V.O. – Meanwhile Satan sends his minions after Anyia, but the angels come to Anyia to warn her of what is to come and she goes into a deep trance. The butterfly on Anyia's neck begins to glow brighter. The clouds became thick and white as snow. The wind began blowing viciously. Dana and Toonie look on in disbelief. Senar seems to understand what is going on. By now Carmen is terrified and Anyia begins to speak as she is literally raised up from her seat and she says......

ANYIA: Father, forgive me for we know not what we do. The time is come for all to bow to the Almighty, the Alpha the Omega, the Lord, my God have mercy on all of those who don't believe.

V.O. "And I saw another mighty angel come down from heaven clothed with a cloud and a rainbow was upon his head and his face was as it were the sun and his feet as pillars of fire."

Rev. 10:1

V.O. – It once was said that you never miss what you had until it's gone. All the everyday struggles that we go through wear on us like a scab, but in some strange way compared to this it will be missed. Senar holds on to Toonie tight, she asked Senar what was wrong with Anyia. Senar looks at her and wipes her eyes and turns and looks at Anyia. No longer in disbelief, he is truly in awe at what he is seeing. Senar pulls over. Carmen gets out the car and walks around to the back passenger seat. She opens the door to help Dana out of the car. Seeing the blood, Carmen tends to Dana. Senar reaches over and touches Anyia's hand and is momentarily pulled in to her vision. He sees the angels coming down from heaven and everything else that comes with it. Momentarily he is horrified. He snatches his hand away and calls out Anyia's name.

EXT. HIGHWAY. NIGHT

SENAR: Anyia is this really happening?

ANYIA: I'm afraid so. It's time, time for us to have peace. The devil can't hurt us anymore.

SENAR: Well tell me what we have to do.

CARMEN: Hello can I have a little help here.

ANYIA: Dana, what happened?

DANA: (Gasping for air) I don't know. My side, it's my side.

SENAR: Blood is everywhere.

V.O. – With all the madness that went on, Dana did not realize she got clawed so bad by the demon she was fighting off. The demon caused hemorrhaging in Dana's side by its sharp claws.

ANYIA: Dana stay with us, help is coming.

SENAR: Everyone, let's help her back in the car.

V.O. – As they walk around to put Dana back in the car, they see Toonie walking beside the car while in a trance. They all turn to see what she was looking at. A two headed beast is coming towards Toonie with foam coming from its mouth. Before Senar could jump forward, Dana steps out in front of Toonie and said to the creature.

DANA: Don't even think about it.

V.O. – While pulling her gun from her back to shoot the creature, Anyia stops Dana and blows the creature away with a blast from her hand.

SENAR: If there's one, I know there are more to come.

ANYIA: Well the score is about to even up soon.

V.O. – Meanwhile they all get back in the car and head towards the coast driving through city after city, seeing carnage everywhere they go. Senar begins to see the whole picture and a sense of calm begins to fall over him. Anyia turns to Senar and puts her hand on his face.

INT. SUV. MIDNIGHT

ANYIA: What's wrong Senar?

SENAR: I'm at peace, but at the same time I'm terrified.

ANYIA: Don't be. Faith has no fear.

V.O. – Just then a louder than ever before clap of thunder rang out and shook the earth from sea to sea. Even the evil one was moved. All who were alive knew that was different than anything they had ever heard before.

"And I will give power unto my two witnesses, and they shall prophecy a thousand two hundred and threescore days clothed in sackcloth."

Rev. 11: 3

ANYIA: That was the first.

SENAR: The first of what?

ANYIA: The first of 7.

SENAR: Oh! Boy!

V.O. - Meanwhile in the Islands, Sarah walks through the brush and gets to a cave on the side of the cliff. She stops to gaze at the water splashing against rocks and remembered the promise of the past,

remembering her daughter she never got to raise because of the burden that she had to carry. It was time for her to come home. She turns to the cave and it begins to light up with a beautiful glow. Now everything was coming full circle. Anyia hears and feels the second of the mighty thunders which shook the earth like a quake. She then turns and looks to the mountains off in the distance and realizes that it is time to go. They all jumped into the truck and headed towards the abandoned private airport that Sheila had told her about long ago.

V.O. - Meanwhile minions that Satan had let loose upon the earth were raging war to find something and they was trying to find it fast. A pocket of survivors were huddled around a barrel of burning wood to keep warm, when they were surrounded by these creatures. They began to scream, but no sound would come out and then they were torn to pieces.

V.O. – Meanwhile at the Vatican, the Pope kneels in front of the altar and begins to pray as the city crumbles around him and he can even hear the screams of the people in the streets. The Pope only a few minutes into a deep prayer, is interrupted by an image before him.

DEMON: Why pray now?

POPE: (The Pope lifts his head up) What do you want from me?

DEMON: I have your seed which has now become mine. By the fornication of your church, you have allowed my son to be.

POPE: What have I done?

DEMON: For your earthly pleasures, I have now come to collect your soul.

V.O. – The Pope begins to pray louder as the demon reaches into his chest and pulls his heart out as it's still beating. The Pope falls to the ground as the demon then takes on the form of the Virgin Mary and proceeds down the corridor.

"Full Circle"

Day Seven

V.O. – Meanwhile as Anyia pulls up to the air strip very slowly, Senar ask Anyia why were they there?

EXT. AIR STRIP. 1 AM

SENAR: Anyia, I have a feeling that you have not told me everything. What's going on now?

ANYIA: It's hard to explain because I am only beginning to understand it myself.

SENAR: Please try to help me understand.

ANYIA: My mother was very special, she was on a river when she was about to give birth to me. As she washed her feet in the water, something grabbed hold of her legs and she began to scream. My grandmother ran to the river only to find my mother being pulled under water by some type of demon. She prayed and rose up an amulet that made the demon burst into flames. She pulled my mother, me and my sister from the water and took her somewhere in the mountains to give birth to us safely. Yes I am a twin. My grandmother said that Kenya would be the beginning and I would be the end. My grandmother went on to say that my mother gave her life protecting me and my sister and we both had a big role to play in God's plan. My sister was left in the wilderness in a cave where she conceived a man child and I was sent away with a man, who most people came to know as my father, but he was not. She also said there were angels guarding the cave until the day came for her to release the amulet that my grandmother had made her swallow. She has been in hiding from that moment on from the evil one who seeks to devour her and the man child. The amulet has something to do with the coming of the Lord, and being my mother's child I am supposed to go to my sister when the time is right, so I can see what it is I am suppose to be doing and what my purpose is in all of this. My grandmother had another daughter and she had three children that I grew up thinking for a long time were my sisters and brother, but they were not.

SENAR: Wow! Ok!

ANYIA: So now you know, and as we speak they are searching for me and my mother. My mother had met a man in the jungle and she conceived me with him and no one but my grandmother knows who he is.

SENAR: So I guess now we are going to fly somewhere right?

ANYIA: (Laughing) You must have been reading my mind.

SENAR: What's so funny?

ANYIA: This is not time to be sad, but happy. We need to head to the islands.

V.O. – As the fish and all the seas began to float on the surface and the water turns to blood all hope seems to be lost, but we know that this must happen in order to fulfill the prophecy. Anyia, Senar, Dana, Carmen and Toonie get in the chopper and fly off towards the islands. Anyia knew that being in the air would make them easy targets, so she said a prayer to the Lord for her and them.

V.O. – Meanwhile standing on a cliff in front of a cave engaged in a vision, the fornicating nun stares into the darkness, glancing at the destruction. Meanwhile on the cliff in front of her cave, Sarah steps to the edge and opens her hands up wide and says in the mighty name of Jesus, let me see the destruction that is to come. Sarah stares into the light that is before her and is able to look right into the eyes of the fornicating nun. Meanwhile on the plane over the ocean, Anyia's butterfly begins to glow and then she is pulled into the same vision as Sarah and the evil one. Just at that moment, both Sarah and the evil nun turns and stares into Anyia's eyes through the vision. Now all can see all.

V.O. - They finally arrived at their destination. Senar was amazed by the beautiful light that shined through the trees. It was like a rainbow with all its beautiful colors. You could see colors change from every angle of the cave. Anyia, being an inexperienced pilot, needed to find a safe place to land. As the others woke up, they could hardly believe what they were seeing. Anyia told everyone that she hoped they are ready for what was about to happen. As they get off the chopper, Anyia sees her grandmother and cousins walking through the grass towards the cave. As they embrace each other, the grandmother directs them to the cave and begins to tell Anyia of her purpose.

EXT. MOUNTAIN TOP. PRE DAWN

SARAH: I knew you were coming.

ANYIA: Well I would have been here sooner, but we had trouble along the way.

TOONIE: Daddy are we dead, cause it feels like heaven here?

CARMEN: Oh my God!

SENAR: I feel it too.

DANA: This is unbelievable.

SARAH: You ain't seen nothing yet.

Senar V.O. - Picture this if you can: High in the mountains close to the clouds and instead of a cool breeze it's a warm breeze; a breeze that holds you and wraps around you as though you are in your mother's womb. Cutting through the brush, there is a trail and on each side of you, there are the most beautiful flowers you would ever see. As Sarah walks ahead, I trail behind just living in the now thanking God for allowing a wretch like me to be in the midst of angels and yet I am not dead. My mama always said the Lord looks out for babies and fools and I haven't been a baby for a long time, but then I was a fool just a week ago. As we go over the hill, we began to see the light even brighter. It was wonderful. I reach over to help Dana. She's really starting to labor from her wound. I put her arm over my shoulder and she says to me....

DANA: Did you ever in your wildest dreams believe that you would be seeing something like this. I mean (Pausing) what is that sitting over there on those rocks?

SENAR: No not ever.

V.O. – There on each side of the cave was a silhouette of two angels sitting upon each rock, and there sat a third on top of the entrance. Toonie jumps in Senar's arms. Sarah turns around to look at the amazement on all their faces. They go over the hill and into the entrance, past the water on the left and right and soft clay running down the middle. Anyia stops in her tracks.

ANYIA: Nana why am I here? Please tell me before I cross these waters.

SARAH: I once told you that your sister was the beginning and you were the end as far as our generational responsibility is concerned. There were many before and will be many after. Today we keep our promise.

ANYIA: To who nana?

SARAH: To God and my Lord Jesus.

V.O. – Everybody stares at them.

ANYIA: What do you mean nana? You know I understand that part of it, but it seems like something is missing.

SARAH: I know for a while you thought that Dena, Rachel, and Michael were your brother and sisters, and then you found out that wasn't the truth, but it was for the good of those that were involved. Your auntie, whose name was Trinity, was my first born. She was attacked by something unnatural in the woods and I fought for her life, but because I knew not what I was fighting I couldn't keep them from getting to my daughter. I had two you know. Your mother fell in love with a man who said he was from somewhere where the waters were always sweet. For a long time he was friends with your mother and our family and you can see the wisdom in his eyes, but you could also see the sadness. You see, he knew that in order to be with your mother he would have to give up something very, very dear to him.

ANYIA: So it was Trinity and my mama Lanee and what did this man have to give up?

SARAH: Yes it was Trinity and your mother and he would have to give up being an angel in order to be with your mother, but one night they became one and he was prepared to be just human because of the love that he had for your mother. Not long after they had finished being one, Lanee was attacked by the same demon who attacked Trinity, but only this time, this man who we call Matthew saved your mother's life from this demon that night. In saving your mother, Matthew lost the battle and he lost his life.

ANYIA: So what happened to my mother?

SARAH: We had to hide her just like we had to hide your sister and she moved on shortly after giving birth to you and Kenya. Lanee is with God now.

ANYIA: Where's my sister?

SARAH: Kenya is in that cave.

ANYIA: Why is she here and I was sent away?

SARAH: Your sister's burden is different than yours and the evil one knows of your sister and that she represents the beginning, but he also knows that your purpose will help usher in his end. I am proud of both of you.

CARMEN: I'm sorry I don't mean to interrupt, but will somebody tell me what that dark cloud is coming in the sky?

SENAR: It sure ain't rain.

DANA: I don't feel so good here.

SARAH: We all need to get inside. We don't have much time.

TOONIE: Daddy I've seen this light before.

INT. CAVE. DAWN

V.O. – The closer that Anyia got to the cave, the brighter the light got. Everybody was speechless. What can you really say at a time like that? As they go through the entrance of the cave, the hair on their necks stands up. Now they can see the angels that are guarding the cave. Two girls greet them dressed in sack cloth. It's Rachel and Dena. A young man appears right behind them. Just over his shoulder there stood a crystal resting place, and there was a woman lying on sheep's wool as peaceful as can be. What was thought to be a dark cloud in reality were the devils minions. They also were attracted to the light.

SENAR: Oh boy! Oh boy! What do we do now?

SARAH: Anyia, quick run to your sister's side. She waits for you. She has something to give you.

V.O. – There lies Kenya as beautiful as the day she was laid to rest.

"And the seventh angel sounded; and there were great voices in heaven, saying, The kingdoms of this world are become the kingdoms of our Lord, and of his Christ; and he Shall reign forever and ever."

Rev. 11:15

V.O. – The demons got closer one right behind the other. Thunder roared and shook the land. The clouds parted and light shone through from heaven and Michael and his angels came through the clouds and made war with the demons. The battle was fierce and unlike anything you can ever imagine. Now the one they call Satan has come in person. Sarah tells Anyia to kneel down at her sister's side and put her hand at her heart and said, "Lord let thy will be done." At that moment Kenya's eyes open wide and stared into Anyia's face. A big smile went across Kenya's face when she realized who Anyia was. Just at that moment, five thunderous booms shook the earth, one right after the other. When it stopped, the rain began to fall.

It was as though the heavens had opened up where we could actually see the war in heaven and as on cue, a great red dragon appeared and the angels fought as we watched helplessly. As the red dragon fought closer to the cave, Dena and Rachel stepped to the entrance of the cave and walked to the cliff side as they hold hands and opened their mouths. Meanwhile, in a cave in the middle of the dessert, the fornicating nun holds her belly in pain as she literally drops to her knees. Surrounded by Satan's minions she lets out a horrible scream. She looks up at the entrance of the cave with tears rolling down her face and sees a snake with red eyes and he says to her, "It's time." As Dena and Rachel become aware of what just happened in the other cave, a fire like no other proceedth out of their mouth and devoured the demons by the thousands and from the east comes a wind like no other wind had blown before. Michael and his angels intercede and fight the red dragon. At that moment, a loud yell came from the cave, a scream like no other. Kenya rises up with her man child still clinging to her breast. The battle goes on as the dragon seeks to devour him. Coming through the brush were two women escorted by two angels dripping with water, their white cloths soaking wet. Sarah realizing it was the spirit of Trinity and Lanee fell to her knees. As their spirit descended upon them, they appeared to their mother and their children as they once were, saying...

TRINITY & LANEE: Don't be afraid my children, for the day has come.

"And I heard a loud voice say in heaven, Now is come salvation and strength and the kingdom of our God."

Rev. 12: 10

SENAR: I'm going to help the girls. We've got to get them in here.

ANYIA: It's you who need their help.

TRINITY & LANEE (Standing over Kenya and her son) They say therefore rejoice ye heavens and ye that dwell in them. Woe to the inhabitants of the earth and of the sea for the devil has come down unto you having great wrath because he knoweth that he hath but a short time. You must leave now it is too dangerous for you to be here now.

SARAH: O Lord Father God please have mercy.

ANYIA: What do we do now Nana?

SENAR: I think we need to get out of here.

TOONIE: Daddy I'm scared.

DANA: Me too baby! Me too!

CARMEN: Is there another way off this mountain?

MICHAEL: Yes there is, but I don't know how safe it is that way either.

V.O. – Dena and Rachel come in to the cave and tell Kenya she must

leave at once. The child in her arms was as calm as a Sunday morning lake, not one tear, not one whimper. As Dana walked past Kenya and the child, she couldn't help but stare into his eyes that looked right through her. Kenya stops; the boy reaches out and puts his hands on Dana and she begins to cry while smiling and then she was not afraid anymore. Her wound was also healed. Kenya then turns around and walks to the back of the cave. As she walks away, she turns and faces them and tells them don't fear for soon he will take all our pain away. She turns around and a giant hole appears in the mountain side from the inside out. Through this hole seems to be another place not of here. Wings sprout from her back and she takes off flying to another place to another land. Three angels fly off with her. Sarah walks over and puts her hand on Dana's shoulder.

DANA: I'm not hurt no more. Oh my God I'm not hurt no more.

SENAR: In all my days of living if everything that I went through was for this one moment I would gladly do it again.

CARMEN: I don't think I ever want to leave this place. After feeling the love and peace of this place, how can we ever go back to anything else?

ANYIA: This peace was only a momentary one. We must follow Michael out of here.

CARMEN: What about Dena and Rachel?

SARAH: He cannot hurt them for they have the power to do great damage while they be witnesses.

EXT. OUTSIDE CAVE. MORNING

V.O. - Dana walks out the front of the cave as if in a daze. She has a smile on her face and you can see the peace within her. She stands at the edge and raises her hands to God while watching the war that goes on around her. Senar runs out after her, but it is too late. She is then swept away by a demon. With all the war that is going on around them Dena and Rachel guard the cave and nothing can get past them. Sarah sits in the cave and says my place is here. For there will be no more peace here on earth for a short while, only a short while.

Chapter Twenty Two
"Almost Home"

V.O. – Meanwhile as the sunrises in the desert, a ghastly scream echoes in the distance. The newborn of the evil one has now arrived, being held by the fornicating nun. She holds up her baby proudly by the cliff side only; to be startled by a vision sent to her by Anyia. The vision was Anyia destroying her baby. Anyia then cracks a smile as she then snaps out of her vision. The fornicating nun turns and runs back to the cave, holding the little evil one. Carmen catches Anyia coming out of her vision.

EXT. JUNGLE. MORNING

V.O. - As Michael leads them through the cave to the jungle below, he stops and tells them he cannot go any further. He must go back to the cave because it is not finished. Anyia, Carmen, Toonie and Senar watch him disappear through the brush. Carmen turns to Anyia.

CARMEN: I guess you'll be leaving soon too. Then what will we do? Where will we go?

ANYIA: Your battle is just beginning.

SENAR: What do you mean?

TOONIE: You're not going to leave us are you?

ANYIA: Only for a short time, but I will be back.

CARMEN: Does anybody know which way to go from here?

SENAR: If only I could have gotten to Dana in time.

ANYIA: She was ready to go, she was at peace and God will look after her now.

CARMEN: Something is coming. I can hear it coming through the bushes.

TOONIE: Me too!

ANYIA: We've got to go now! Come on this way.

SENAR: How do we get off this island?

ANYIA: Once we get off the island we will be safer, but not safe.

CARMEN: What island is this?

ANYIA: San Miguel, there should be a boat on the other side of that hill. Let's go.

SENAR: I thought no one lived on this island.

CARMEN: You and I both thought wrong.

V.O. - As they go down the hill, they can still hear something coming through the brush behind them. They begin to run towards the dock, but before they can get on the boat, one of the demons leaps out and grabs Carmen. Anyia turns and raises her hand. The demon splits Carmen's throat wide open and then burst into flames from Anyia's blast. Senar grabs Toonie and tells Anyia to run to the boat because something else is coming. Anyia not wanting to leave Carmen behind; calls out her name and then runs back and kneels over her. She prays silently to the Lord while Senar and Toonie call out her name in the background. She hears nothing but her own prayer. Senar runs back, just as she is finished praying.

SENAR: Come on Anyia. We have to go.

V.O. – Senar, Anyia and Toonie turn and run to the boat but another demon is there standing in between them and the boat. Anyia and Senar raise their guns to kill the demon, but just then Toonie grabs Carmen's pump shotgun off the ground and runs between Senar and Anyia. She pumps the shotgun one time then says.

TOONIE: I'm tired of running. Y'all killed my mama and almost everybody else I've come to love.

SENAR: Toonie!

ANYIA: Give me the gun baby.

TOONIE: Pop goes the weasel.

V.O. – Toonie pumps and shoots the shotgun until there are no bullets left. Senar runs and grabs the shotgun and says, "He's dead baby, he's dead." Anyia looks at Senar and says, "Did you teach her that." As they get into the boat, Anyia puts a barrier around them and heads towards the coast. They get off in Ventura and start to look around for a truck, car or anything to get them to a safe place, but little did they know that nowhere was safe.

V.O. - Meanwhile back on the island, Sarah, Michael, Dena and Rachael hold hands and form a circle to protect the doorway that Kenya and her child went through. Their power combined prevents anything or anyone from entering at all.

V.O. - Meanwhile Anyia has the amulet in her pocket and she begins to get sick at the stomach. Not knowing what is wrong, Senar begins to worry. She knows that her time is coming and she feels as though she will not be able to protect them any longer. They find a car and hot wire it. Senar jumps in the driver seat and Toonie gets in the middle. Anyia gets in the passenger seat and they head towards L.A. That's where the people that are still alive are going, but something else is waiting too! Once in L.A they see that mayhem has taken over and there is a man speaking to a mass group of people and he is saying all types of things against God and healing wounds on himself and other people. Anyia's neck starts to glow and she knows what this is that he is speaking. The man is a big man, his eyes are dark and his hands are red with blood. He is making people bow down to him or die.

EXT. ALLEY. OUTSIDE CAR. DAY

ANYIA: Senar I want you to promise me something.

SENAR: What's that?

ANYIA: That you will keep the faith and remember the things that you have witnessed.

SENAR: I promise.

TOONIE: I miss Carmen daddy, and I need to know that she is with God in heaven.

SENAR: She is with God baby and she feels no pain.

ANYIA: We need to get away from here, it's not safe.

SENAR: Then where do we go?

ANYIA: There is nowhere to go here on earth.

SENAR: I must say my life has changed a lot since that cookout HUH!

ANYIA: I'm sure it has. You play a big part in all of this.

TOONIE: I think we should go now!

V.O. – Just then their car is surrounded by the followers of the demon who poses as a man. They began to break the windows and reach into the car. Anyia exudes a tremendous amount of energy that blows them away. Senar hit's the gas and then hits the brakes. He stops and gets out of the car; he turns and looks at the big man standing alone with dead demons all around him. The big man walks towards him slowly. Anyia gets out of the passenger side.

SENAR: So this is the one they talked about Huh!

ANYIA: I am afraid so.

DEMON: Stay awhile, I'm about to cook out.

ANYIA: I think not.

SENAR: Yeah all your food taste bad.

V.O. – The demon goes to rush them. Two angels swoop down and begin to slice and dice him. The demon turns to run as he summons more of his minions. Senar and Anyia run to the car. Before he could pull off, the sun is blotted out by thousands upon thousands of angels. The war in heaven is now fully here on earth. Senar and Anyia speed off to the north side of town. Senar can see that Anyia is throwing up her guts out of the window. They pull over and exit the car. Just then a thunderstorm appeared from nowhere and the skies got dark. As

Anyia looks down the street, her neck begins to glow. Looking down the street, Senar can see images coming, through the rain. For the first time, not only did Anyia's neck glow, but her eyes began to glow also. It was as though she became a phoenix. As the figures got closer, Anyia could see that it was the fornicating nun and her baby with hundreds of demons in front of her. Seeing Anyia, the fornicating nun stopped in her tracks as she remembered the vision. Holding her ground; feeling safe among her demons, she laughed at Anyia. Out of nowhere, 7,770 angels appeared in front of Anyia and Senar along with Michael the Arch Angel.

MICHAEL THE ARCH ANGEL: Your faith has stood well and you, he is pleased.

V.O. - Anyia falls down to her knees looking to the sky and thanking God in Jesus name.

MICHAEL THE ARCH ANGEL: Many battles have been lost, but with the blood of the lamb we have won the war in Jesus name. Go forth; you know what you must do. We are here with you always.

V.O. - Anyia took off running towards the nun straight to the demons in front of her. Senar called out her name, but she would not stop. The angels went before her clearing a path of death and destruction straight to the nun. Anyia runs through the path pulling two knives from her back. Anyia gets within 10 feet of the nun and jumps high in the air and throws both knives that were blessed by the Holy Spirit, straight through the nun. Satan swoops down and grabs the baby as Michael and some of his army flies off behind him. She lands right over the nun and stands in front of her and says, "Who's laughing now?" She turns and runs back towards the car where Senar and Toonie are waiting. She is very weakened, so Senar runs and grabs her and carries her to the top floor of the building that they entered. He puts Anyia on the floor on top of his shirt that he has just ripped off. Toonie starts to cry, not knowing what is wrong with Anyia. Senar is worried too!

EXT. ROOF TOP. DUSK

SENAR: Anyia what is wrong with you.

ANYIA: I have one last thing to do and then it's in your hands to do the right thing.

SENAR: And what might that be?

ANYIA: You will know when it's time and the spirit will lead you.

TOONIE: Get up Anyia, we need you.

ANYIA: You only need the Lord and he is always there.

SENAR: They're coming, I can hear them.

ANYIA: There's not much time, take this.

SENAR: Why are you giving me this?

ANYIA: It's what they are coming for.

TOONIE: Daddy, look out!

V.O. – Senar shoots everything and everybody coming through the door. He puts Anyia on his shoulder and grabs Toonie's hand, then heads to the roof. He barricades the door and lays Anyia back down. He gives Toonie a gun which in any other circumstance would be child endangerment, but in this case he just wanted to save her life. Anyia sees something more powerful coming and begins to pray for the world as she stands to her feet on her own. As she raises her hands to God, a beast breaks through the door. The heavens open up and a light shines down on her. She turns and looks at Senar and smiles.

ANYIA: I love you Senar and I will see you again. I cherished every moment that we shared together and I love you too Toonie. Take this and it will protect you when I am gone.

V.O – She closes his hand around the amulet.

SENAR: I love you too! Please don't leave me now, I just found you and I don't want to lose you.

ANYIA: You won't.

TOONIE: Please don't go.

V.O. – The Demon walks up to Anyia, she turns to face him and she stares into his eyes and begins to pray. The butterfly on her neck turns to fire because of the presence of evil in front of her. She raises her hand and rips the beast down the middle then she jumps into the bowels of the beast. There was a tremendous explosion and guts went all over the place and all the beast with him blew up too! Now there was an eerie silence on the roof and Toonie was crying uncontrollably. Senar puts his hand on her face, while tears run down his face and tells her something in her ear.

SENAR: No matter what happens to me I want you to be strong and remember everything that you've seen here.

TOONIE: But I'm just a little girl.

SENAR: With a big heart.

TOONIE: Something is coming again.

SENAR: Listen baby swallow this and close your eyes and you will be ok.

TOONIE: You promise.

SENAR: I do.

V.O. – Toonie goes into a deep sleep and there seems to be a force around her. Senar grabs his guns in both hands and looks over the roof. There were demons and people that had bowed down to the beast and they are coming for Senar and Toonie. He found a place to hide Toonie and ran down the stairs to confront them on a different floor, so they would not know where Toonie was at. As they came for him and ripped at him, he shot, cut, kicked, and fought until he was out of ammo and strength. He returned to the roof only to find Toonie gone from the place he had left her. He screams out her name, but gets no answer. He begins to cry and pray. He huddles up in the corner of the roof. He has nothing left; he's tired, alone and hurt gravely. He seems to be talking to someone that is not visible to no one but him. He picks himself up and falls back down again flat on his face. Barely conscious he looks up and there is a demon standing there who puts his foot on Senar's back. Senar is helpless, but turns over and laughs at the beast and then says.

EXT. ROOF TOP. SUN DOWN

SENAR: Run, enjoy the beach while you can because your time is short and I know the end of this story, so do what you want with me. I have seen the glory of God and it is beautiful.

DEMON: Where is the girl?

SENAR: Go to hell, OOPS! My bad, that's exactly where you're going.

V.O. – The demon picks him up, holds him high in the air then opens his mouth. Senar pulls out a grenade and sticks his whole hand in the creature's mouth with the grenade. The beast bites down, the bomb goes off, blowing the creatures head off along with Senar's hand. Bleeding badly, he crawls over to the corner of the building and ties a rag around his wrist to slow the bleeding.

Chapter Twenty Three
"I See the Glory"

SENAR V.O. – As I sit here bleeding to death knowing that I have but a few minutes to live, everything seems to be going by in a flash, but that is how I remember everything happening. For some reason now I know why I was born and I can still hear them coming, but it don't matter now. I have seen the glory of my God and Lord please forgive me for my sins, and mama I'm sorry please forgive me. You were right, in the Mighty name of Jesus. AMEN

V.O. – Senar see's the beast and his minions walking towards him, he knows his fight is over, he's dying anyway, so he stares up at the sky and he sees Anyia walking from the other direction. He grins, but he can't say a word. She speaks, but her mouth is not moving, she is just a spirit of herself. Time stands still and she walks up to him and say's…

ANYIA: I told you I would be back when your time has come and now you will feel no pain and what they do to your body can never happen

to your soul. My father's house has many mansions and many rooms. Come with me Senar.

V.O. – Senar takes his last breath then his spirit leaves with Anyia. At that moment, time returns to normal and they rip his body apart.

V.O. – Meanwhile two angels sit on a rock on a cliff on the island of Bermuda. Inside there is a woman with a little boy. Two more angels appear with a little girl in their arms. They lay her down next to the woman and the boy. The woman walks over to the girl and begins to pray. She wakes up and opens her eyes and begins to cry, not understanding what is going on, she began to cry out for her daddy, just then a vision of Senar and Anyia appear to her saying, "Rest my child, we will see you soon."

V.O. – Toonie sits up calling her daddy's name until she see's Kenya.

EXT. CLIFF IN BERMUDA. NIGHT

KENYA: Go back to sleep my child for your time has yet to come. You and my son have many wonderful things to do. You will be safe here until then. I will lie down next to the both of you to wait for our time to come, but for now; just for now, my cousins must witness and the devil must have his time on earth. The end is just beginning, and the new beginning will be here soon. There is much yet to happen for now we will sleep. Our battle has just begun.

V.O. "And behold I come quickly; and my reward is with me, to give every man according as his work shall be. I am the Alpha and the Omega, the beginning and the end, the first and the last."

Revelations 22:12, 13

V.O. - A dove slowly flies away from the cave straight into the heavens; watching the war which rages on.

V.O. "And I saw a new heaven and a new earth: for the first heaven and the first earth were passed away; and there was no more sea."

REV. 21:1